Autumn Equinox

Autumn Equinox

By Jabbour Douaihy

Translated by Nay Hannawi

The University of Arkansas Press
Fayetteville
2001

Front cover photograph by Dee Coghlan

Library of Congress Cataloging-in-Publication Data

Duwayhi, Jabur.
   [I'tidal al-kharif. English]
   Autumn equinox / by Jabbour Douaihy ; translated by Nay Hannawi.
     p. cm.
   ISBN 1-55728-707-4 (pbk. : alk. paper)
     I. Hannawi, Nay, 1976– II. Title.

PJ7820.U92 I8513 2001
892.7'36—dc21

                                        2001035234

For,
Thérèse

Autumn Equinox

Saturday, May 30, 1986

Today, I suddenly realized as I was turning the pages of the Heritage Society calendar, that I've always had an image of the sequence of the seasons on an old and fixed blueprint. It's a straight line starting at the beginning of October and continuing straight till the end of June, where it turns back in the form of a rainbow to meet with the beginning of the straight line at the end of September. The distance between October and the end of the year, that is autumn, seems very small compared to the lighted part of the year, extending until the end of spring. I brought this up with my friends at the café on Al-Midan Square, and one of them confessed that he imagines the days of the week in the form of a closed circle, starting on Monday morning and ending on Sunday evening. That comforted me a little, and as soon as I went back home, I asked my sister if this meant anything to her. She said, without raising her head from her knitting, that the week for her is a flight of stairs, descending one step every day, Thursday being the only landing dividing them, but she didn't understand why. She asked me why I was asking her this kind of question.

Before sunset, we heard echoes of an Israeli air raid on one of the refugee camps near the seashore. Some children from the neighborhood climbed up to the roofs

3

of the buildings and started shouting, "Look. There's the smoke!" Then the planes disappeared, and the children climbed down. The ambulance sirens and antiaircraft machine guns could still be heard in the distance. Some people say that the teenagers who guard the camp take the opportunity to fire the antiaircraft machine guns, which they stand behind night and day.

Wednesday, June 3, 1986

Yesterday, I wrote Lara a letter. As usual, I don't know when she'll receive it or even when it will be mailed. I took it to the travel agency today, and the manager promised to send it with the next person flying to the United States.

I get all excited when I write to Lara. Her grandmother is Polish. She told me that the second time we met, without my asking her, and she added that she had inherited "the Mediterranean flame," as she called it, from her playful father who left her mother lonely and desperate in one of the southern villages of France. And when I asked her about her native country, she laughed loudly and flung herself at me, and after a little while, she told me she was from New York, but she dreamt of traveling to Greece to follow in Henry Miller's footsteps. She said she was glad she'd met me.

I told her that I came from an ageless mountain village and that in the consciousness of my people there was no memory of any migrations except for winter moves to their other village near the shore, which shyly overlooks the sea. It was as if they hadn't come from anywhere, as if they'd sprouted there, sheltered by the sky and the walnut trees on the shoulder of that deep valley inhabited by fog and hermits who had been passing down the land for generations and fighting over it steadily and stubbornly. They didn't trust books with their history, not because they had nothing to tell, but because all the details of the past centuries still loomed in their lives. They had been telling their story for thousands of years and passing it on to each other according to the same narrative they all knew by heart, and the day they put it in writing would be the beginning of their end.

Lara laughed again and said she loved me. She said she loved the way I spoke English and didn't believe a word I said. I think that was the same day when she suddenly got quiet, stared at me, and shouted, "Oh my God! He looks like M.F.! He looks like M.F. Ever since I saw you the first time, I've been wondering who you looked like." And the next time we met, she held up a book with M.F.'s picture and told me, "If you added a mustache to the picture, it would be you." But we dropped the

5

subject. Perhaps seeing me so often after that made her quit comparing me to anyone.

I felt some vanity when Lara compared me to M.F., not because he was handsome and attractive in his youth and mystery surrounded his relationships with women, but because Lara made me imagine, for the first time in my life, the possibility of moving one step in the other direction, even if through somebody else's reflection— to transform myself, even if hypothetically, from being the reader and the viewer who I thought I'd always be, to the actor of an active role, which somebody else was watching.

I wrote her a long letter, the tenth, I believe, since I'd come back from America. An average of one letter per season. I didn't wait for an answer from her, since she had no way of sending letters. In the months that followed my return, we talked several times on the phone, but international lines were no longer possible, and when I heard at the beginning of the year that the lines had been reconnected, I tried several times, but every time I got an automated voice saying the number I had dialed was out of service.

I told her in my letter yesterday that I was a little nervous; I had shaved my mustache—the one I used to curl up like those of my frowning uncles and grand-fathers in the pictures on the wall, and I was afraid of looking at my naked face. And I told her that I now took rapid glances at it from a good distance from the mirror and scolded myself. I also told her I intended to change a lot of things about my life, but I was at the same time afraid of meddling with any part of myself for fear of total collapse. I might collapse and drown in sorrows I couldn't bear. I wrote her all these things—and whom else would I tell?—because she always used to say that we had something in common, which she called, *"la fragilité française."*

I don't think I'll see Lara again. I don't know if she will receive my letter. Sometimes, travelers just throw away the letters instead of posting them; and then, Lara might have moved to another address or maybe to another country. So why do I still find myself trying to seduce her with this soft and vulnerable talk every time I write to her?

Wednesday, June 10, 1986

My aunt came to visit us at noon. She showered my sister and me with kisses as she always does whenever we get together.

It seems that my aunt doesn't distribute her love equally among her brothers, and all she has ever allocated to us is a small portion of it. From my side, all I ever saw in her was her lively loving face, which always asked how we were doing, yet her continuous and excessive enthusiasm had something of a mother's worrying and yearning. Perhaps in her mind my sister and I were still too young, so she kept her true feelings from us because indifference and hatred were the business of adults. She still smelled of that old-fashioned powder. I wondered where she could buy it these days. I used to see the powder on sale in Souad's fabric store in our old neighborhood—a wooden box with flower designs and maybe Chinese writing. We were flooded with this scent whenever she bent over us, while we worked diligently with our books and notebooks in that dark room of the old house. My mother never let us open the window overlooking the river and the orange grove. Our aunt would kiss us and say in what sounded like a whisper, "Pay attention to your studies and to your souls." At that time I didn't need to be reminded of my schoolwork. As for our "souls," in my mind the word was like an expensive and cracked urn that should be held with great care.

My mother was apprehensive after my aunt's visit. They had a tacit understanding and a secret exchange of signs that was as old as my mother's coming into my father's family. My aunt didn't attend my parents' wedding, she wasn't in the wedding picture, and it seems that the reconciliation must have taken place the day I was baptized and she became my godmother. She was beautiful, my aunt; she looked like the sad actress Irene Papas, at least in the picture where she's holding me with my eyes shut, crying as the priest pours the baptismal water on my head. If it's true that my aunt would have never been admitted in our house if I'd been a girl instead of a boy, then I was the reason behind her smile in the baptismal picture. So, it was a sincere smile. I worry about my aunt and how I should feel toward her, and sometimes I feel as if I would be betraying my mother if I followed my impulse to like her.

Although my aunt didn't talk about anything in particular, she urged me, as usual, to get married. I am already over thirty, and I am my parents' only son—and there are only few males in our family—but when she kissed my sister and me again and left, my mother sighed and prayed, "God protect us from the evil of the coming days." Then she asked me to come home early and not drive around too long.

I returned around seven and sat by myself on the balcony; I remembered Lara and her loud laugh. Lara's enthusiasm about life was beyond me. It was a pretty evening, with that blend of enchanting sunset light and soft breeze that makes life so enjoyable you wish it would last forever. I listened to the voices of the town fade, and I quietly reflected on my own death.

Thursday, June 11, 1986

Brother Shafiq's procession passed in front of our house. As usual he walked barefoot and was followed by a crowd of young men and women, chanting and praying. Among them, I recognized Lutfi—my friend who works at the projector in Cinéma Royale across the street from our house. Some handicapped people were in the procession, too.

These are people who refuse to become hermits or withdraw from life, but instead they visit the sick and the old. They perform their prayers alone and allow girls to read St. Paul's sermons and only chant old Syriac tunes. I'm sure Lutfi wishes I'd join them. My mother told me Uncle Mansour also came to visit us this afternoon, and as usual, he stood at the door and asked only for me, then left refusing to even come in for coffee. My mother looked hard at me and measuring her words carefully, she said, "Sometimes I'd rather you left again."

Saturday, June 13, 1986

They cut down the lilac tree today. I was expecting it. It had been a hot topic among the neighbors for weeks—no, for months. My sister was watering the hortensia in the window sill and on the balcony, announcing her schedule for tomorrow, Sunday: "I'll call

Antoinette as soon as I wake up; it's her birthday tomorrow. It'll make her happy because she doesn't expect me to know when her birthday is. After that, I'll go to mass. I hope we don't get Father Joachim again this Sunday—half an hour of preaching against short skirts and the enemies of Lebanon—because I also have to visit my aunt before lunch—I promised—or else she'll be upset. In the afternoon . . ." My sister suddenly stopped twittering and pointed toward the street, calling to me, "Look! They cut down the tree."

They call it Sitt Emily's tree—Sitt Emily is the mayor's wife. It's a tall and lanky tree called the "Indian Lilac," I think. Its flowers bloom the first week of May, bringing color to our dull skies for several weeks. People say the lady with the sad face ordered it by mail from a professional French gardening magazine. Twenty small plants arrived by plane, and Sitt Emily planted them with her own hands on both sides of the street during a public ceremony and supervised watering them and taking good care of them. She had a different hat to wear for each day of the week, and she also had the first word in matters concerning the municipality. She was behind the project to spray mosquitoes using a huge pump mounted on a jeep; it let out thick white clouds that the children followed and walked into, inhaling the spray and singing. Around twenty people got asthma as a result. Sitt Emily's husband used to praise her views in public and then give her a taste of various methods of torture in private, so she took off to Brazil on a short visit and hasn't come back. The mayor has been in deep and continuous sorrow since, and people who know him say he often cries; he doesn't attend mass, and instead he stays at home polishing his wife's shoes, arranging them in rows and sitting down to watch them.

The goats and new buildings ate up all the lilac trees except one, this huge tree spreading its branches in every direction; its buds bloom the first week of May and add a special flavor to the days. Its branches have spread everywhere and its roots have sprouted in every direction till they surfaced inside the Sayeghs' house, pulling out the tiles. Afraid it would harm the foundations of the house, the owners filed a complaint at the town hall, but nobody followed up on it. Today, they got an electric saw and tied the tree with ropes from all sides because they couldn't predict to which side it would fall. They blocked the traffic in the main street, slowly brought it down to the ground, and sent it far away on a big truck.

In the afternoon, I went to my room and lay on my bed till the evening with a cloud of melancholy over my head. I'll start tomorrow . . . or on Monday, the day after tomorrow at the latest.

Sunday, June 14, 1986

I don't know why this Sunday I gave in to my sister's repeated requests that I should go with her to mass. Syriac hymns still fill me with ecstasy. And the Church of Our Lady—who is barefoot in the picture and surrounded by a flock of rosy-cheeked cherubs—is still the most peaceful and comforting place in the world to me, where I surrender to myself, or even to sleep, without fear. Why don't I come here more often when the Sunday and holiday crowds are not around and I can be alone under the gaze of the saints amidst the scent of incense?

After mass I waited for my sister near the women's door. I must have stood in the same spot where Uncle Raffoul got shot. The bullet hit his gun tucked in his waistband; then people dragged him into the church. I have experienced the incidents of our family in the form of news about places that I knew and others I didn't know, places I always went to (getting directions when necessary) and stood in riveted there. The first to die was Abu-Saeed, whom my father's uncle attacked with a knife on the Feast of the Transfiguration in 1946. He fell on the village square under the second sycamore, in front of the door of the bakery. The women hurried to cover him with a white sheet, but he was still alive. He cursed them as his soul painfully languished, and he

13

tried to get up, but fell dead. The bakery has been closed for years. He was avenged seven years later at the street corner that leads down to the river. There my aunt's husband lay dead for two hours, bullets showering down from all sides. Then the shooting finally stopped when Father Antoun intervened, coming from the side of the school, shouting until his screams drowned out the whizzing of bullets—so it was said. He called to the people on both sides by name, making them stop. And in front of Cinéma Royale, next to the house we now live in, Uncle Raffoul lay in wait for his rival Yusef and ordered him to turn back, but he didn't. So my uncle emptied a gun with ten bullets into his body, but Yusef didn't die. At home, I heard all sorts of things about our enemies, but I don't remember anyone saying they were cowards.

Monday, June 15, 1986

I woke up eager and tense, like a runner at the starting line waiting for the gun to go off. I began by collecting the green pencils made in Germany. I had been in the habit of scattering them all over my table and forgetting them in drawers or between the pages of books I'd been reading; I would buy them by the dozen, always choosing B and B2 pencils. I had experimented for more than a week before deciding on this brand. The Berol type B is hard enough for tentative drafts, whereas the B2 is necessary for the final versions. I always stockpiled more of these pencils than I could possibly use; perhaps because I was always afraid the bookstores would run out of them. I am still amazed that these pencils are always available, when we often run out of gasoline and flour.

I gathered the pencils on the table, broke them up into little pieces, and threw them into the garden. Then I turned to my spiral notebooks and started tearing up the pages I had written on. But I kept thinking of the broken pencils under my window, so I went out to the garden and picked them up from among the gardenias and from under the shady thick branches of the olive tree, which has refused to bear fruit ever since my father built the house next to it, ever since we asked to be its neighbors. I picked up the wooden pieces patiently, one by one, searching the grass so that no trace of them would remain under my window. I gathered them and hid them behind the trunk of the pomegranate tree my grandmother planted in my name at the edge of the garden. She used to always remind me to let no one come near it: "Only you can pick the fruits of this tree when they mature." And she repeated the prohibition to my mother and sister.

After lunch I drove my car over to the old narrow

stone bridge and threw my pencils into the river. I had to throw them into where the water was moving so that I would completely lose sight of them. Today I also got rid of the erasers.

I nibbled away at some of them into tiny bits and left the rest under the seats of Cinéma Royale, where I went this afternoon to watch a movie, *La Femme d'à Côté*. When I got back, I gave the spiral notebooks I'd been saving to Abu-Hanna, the old grocery store owner, who could use them to record the neighbors' accounts at his store.

All I kept was this thick notebook, the one I am writing in now, with a picture of a redheaded French cabaret dancer on the cover. Lara gave it to me when she said goodbye at the airport. After giving her a long kiss, I picked up my carry-on and walked toward the gate, leafing through the notebook for some excuse to turn back and see Lara one last time. I thought it was a book, but its first pages were blank, so I flipped through it and tried to quickly see the rest. The whole book was blank. I turned back to Lara, and she called, laughing loudly, "Fill it with those wild fantasies of yours and don't forget to mention me."

Friday, June 19, 1986

I should continue what I started on Monday. I've

already planned what I intend to do down to the smallest details. I've even gone so far as to write down what I want to do on the last pages of an address book I keep in the inside pocket of my suit coat. All my intentions are embodied in those French sentences in slender handwriting and red ink that I purposefully chose. As I carefully inscribed them, I promised myself the pleasure I would feel when I saw these resolutions in the imperative mode transformed into real actions ("Destroy the writing tools . . . Change the decor of the room . . ."). And I predicted that, preceding this pleasure, there would be the usual anxiety and fear I have inherited from that white school on the shoulder of the city market, where very tall men with blue eyes who were dressed in black and whose names were Ambroise or Albert—the angels—took turns in teaching us austerity.

So I planned everything and waited. I waited for some important event to happen and strike one of the pillars of our life—something I dared not imagine, falling on us. I could see myself taking advantage of some form of chaos and noise in order to start. I needed a starting point, some kind of introduction, but no such thing happened. The battles had moved away from us years ago and had become limited to the capital and its suburbs. Of course, there was the constant threat of being kidnapped or robbed, or even of a car bomb. But nothing. So I decided to get moving the day the Sayeghs cut down the lilac tree that Sitt Emily had planted. And for five days now, I've been free from writing, from that unbearable burden. Writing used to occupy my thoughts all day and parts of the night, too, but I didn't sit at my desk except for a couple of hours in the afternoon. That's because I used to be scared in the evening and unmotivated in the morning when I would go down to the garden to the new flowers I'd planted. I would caress these flowers and blow on them to help them grow, guiding the ivy along the western wall of the garden, measuring how high it had grown. I watched the sudden blossoming of roses and gardenias, which we offered in bouquets to the neighbors. I love our small garden before sunrise, how it embraces us and fences in our sleep. News about battles used to shake me up, and I would run into my room. But on quiet days, I would roam the coffee shops with friends and would be sucked in by the gossiping and laughing. The smallest details distracted me: my sister's or my mother's absence from the house disabled me. I needed to know that they were there, behind the door, even if I couldn't hear them, my sister laughing and my mother sighing as she told about the misery she's suffered ever since she came into our father's family or shedding a few tears as she told stories about her brother Rafael, my uncle, the bachelor.

I usually started with the title. I would write it several times and stare at it, waiting. I strove for beginnings, for the image, for the origin, so I wrote about people, my people, who don't know how to stand up straight, who move in interrupted rhythms with their backs bent toward the ground and walk as if they have a weight around their necks. I talked about them in the past, a tribe that set its tents at the barren foot of one of the mountains. And there came a dawn when whispers were heard and a commotion crashing like a wave against the tents in the quarter from one end to another. And there he appeared, in the prime years of manhood, crowds of people all around him and all kneeling on the ground, eyes looking upward at him from toe to head. Their gazes were a mixture of wonder and provocation. He stood tall in the middle of the road as no human had stood before. He hit the surface of the ground as a perpendicular line touches the horizontal, straight as a skewer, impeccable, unbent. His eyes had a brilliant calm and warmth. There was a certain harmony and perfect balance in the distribution of the upward propelling energy between every muscle and every joint of his body, and the gravity of the Earth. My people were attracted to the blaze of his walk—as though they were almost starting to pull out of their bent posture, though not having enough courage to stand as tall as he stood. They had some slowness and humbleness that soon brought them back to the ground.

He did not stop, but pointed far off and disappeared into a fold in the mountain.

My notebooks were full of similar stories under the titles, *The Tribes of the Narrow Land* or *Souls with No Gardens.* They were stories of a time past. I used to think that everything had been decided back then, that everything had already happened, and that nothing worth mentioning has happened since. Besides these, there were stories about more recent times, but they, too, revolved around themselves like an echo. And when I got tired, I used to relax in "poetic" moments:

Before sunrise
Birds twittered
Abundantly;
I am asleep,
My bed is wooden,
My table stands calmly
On its four legs.

I used to write things and hide them in the drawer of my closet, which was filled with books that spilled into the living room and sometimes into the kitchen. My sister would rearrange the books, and I would scatter them again until she screamed at me. I would promise for the last time to arrange them, and she would make fun of my promise. I used to read my stories to some of my friends, but I didn't like how they always liked them. It's been a while since I've quit doing that. The stories stayed in the drawer, where I returned to them every once in a while, measuring their gradual fading with the passage of time until I got rid of them last Monday. At least I got rid of the guilt that haunted me every day I did not hold a pencil.

I don't know how I ended up writing even though I grew up in a family where there was no trace of anything written except the legal documents that my grandmother kept under her bed. My grandmother called me in from to time to time to carefully read these documents so that I would know that we had, for example, the right to pass through the orange grove next to the river, or that we owned eight hundred shares of the barren land right next to our old house in Virgin Mary's quarter. There's no doubt that my mother was the first to introduce books into my father's family. She brought them, as she says, with her wedding trousseau, together with the filigreed china tea set she had inherited from her mother and now promises to my sister. She kept her books from St. Joseph's School—a copy of the Bible, and some stories about melancholic love by Gibran Khalil Gibran that my uncle Rafael gave her. And until recently, she still put on her glasses to read to us in a loud and steady voice the story of Martha al Baniyya, the woman who fell in love with the mysterious knight that she met at the well.

Monday, June 22, 1986

Uncle Mansour called me. It was the first time I ever heard his voice on the phone. I found it strange, different maybe, because coming through the phone, it was just a voice, unaccompanied by the facial expressions that Uncle Mansour uses when he speaks. I also wondered how he agreed to speak through a device that he couldn't control. He was also brief on the phone. But his voice was loud, maybe because he didn't know exactly how much he needed to raise it to be heard. He said that he would like to see me and asked me to be careful. I reminded him that the war was far off. He explained that it had nothing to do with the war. He was going to visit us soon to talk to me. My mother was in the kitchen; my sister was on the balcony listening to "Radio Love" and watching the street traffic. Neither heard the phone ring, and I didn't tell them what Uncle Mansour said. My mother nags me with enough questions and warnings every time I step out the door.

I have to set a time with Lutfi, so he can help me find a picture of M.F.; Najib Al-Bahri, the owner of Cinéma Royale, keeps all the old posters and banners in a closet under the wooden stairs that lead up to Lutfi's projection room.

Wednesday, June 24, 1986

I woke up early today to some strange noises and clamor outside our house. I got dressed in a hurry and went out to the balcony. Surrounding our garden were more than twenty young men and women, and in front of each was a wooden easel; they were students of the Fine Arts Institute. Their teacher, who wore a big straw hat, had chosen our house and its garden for them to paint as their examination in oil painting.

A little later, Nirmal came running into the garden. He lives with three other Indian workers in a nearby building that is under construction. He is known in the neighborhood because, unlike his peers, he agrees to work after his official hours, doing small services here and there, teaching the women to cook curried food and bringing them spices of unknown origin. He comes over to our house without us asking and takes out the shears and prunes the rose bushes in our garden. Today he came in a big hurry. He must have left work claiming that he needed to take care of the roses in order to get here at such an early hour. But he stood there, in front of the house, next to the pomegranate tree, looking at the male and female students of the Fine Arts Institute and smiling. (Nirmal is the only Indian among his peers who smiles. They are always scolding him in their language, and he listens silently: his lighthearted attitude probably shames his people).

He stood for a long time in front of the pomegranate tree, motionless. He insisted on smiling the whole time, and if he accidentally let his face muscles relax, he would make sure to show some of his white teeth again, probably because he thought of himself as posing in front of a cameraman and he needed to smile; this way he would be ready if one of the students decided to include him in his painting. Then every once in a while, he looked right or left to make sure that he was still standing within the whole frame of the house and the garden and moved a step or two in order to remain in the middle of what he considered to be the boundaries of the painting. As for the students, they were more involved with their painting materials—the brushes, the tubes, and the paint—than they were with our house and garden, as if it were the first time they had gotten to apply what they had learned so far only theoretically. They consulted each other and called out to the teacher when they got a color they thought was appropriate, fascinated the whole time with this new chemistry. It was clear that they were all busy with the details of the smears of oil paint they were adding to the white canvas stretched in front of them and were incapable of paying attention to the subject of the painting and the manner of painting it at the same time.

And so half an hour passed with none of them noticing Nirmal's movements. And then I thought I'd better leave the smiling Indian alone because I didn't want to be here on the balcony at the end of the session when he raced over, searching for his face in the students' paintings. When I came back home, my sister told me that when the sun beat down on them, Nirmal went around giving everyone bottles of cold water and then hurried back to his spot. At noon, none of the Fine Arts Institute students had included Nirmal in their paintings. But in spite of that, when the teacher signaled for them to finish, Nirmal helped them bring down their easels, shook hands with them one by one, and waved a long goodbye as they walked away.

Ten days have passed since I stopped writing. The amount of time isn't important in itself, since weeks and months used to go by when I wouldn't write a single line or would write things I didn't want to keep. What's important is that ten days have passed since I gave up the idea of writing—meaning that I'll be able to go on with my life without writing. I fear this weakness—this loss of immunity and safety. Will I get used to life as such, without an intermediary, a life from which writing has left with no return, with no trace? Is the thing I've always been afraid of now happening to me, the thing I mentioned in my last letter to Lara, the one I doubt she's

25

gotten? Speaking of Lara, I need a woman like her—part belligerent, part compassionate—a woman who can be sarcastic and loving at the same time. Mary cares about different things. I am fond of her, but she speaks a different language. Mary can't help me with what I'm going through. Why do I keep wandering off and regurgitating these thoughts? I shouldn't look back or stop at what others may say about me. I shouldn't hesitate in carrying out my plan. Postponing it doesn't help me at all.

I went to my room early this evening because I was determined to clean it up, before the day was over. First I lined the table against the wall so when I sit down at it I won't be facing the closet mirror that reflects the part of the city where the ships dock. Here too, I had needed some time to plan out an order which would allow me to constantly see—not the nakedness of lonely waters—but an inhabited sea, a sea crowded with the same ships we observed for years and years on our way to school.

The ride to school was a daily trial. Students from our town and from neighboring villages used to push into that old bus where their screaming crammed in with the bags rolling in the aisles and the driver's warnings to keep our hands off the windows, lock the rear door, and sit so that he could drive his vehicle safely. And often, the driver would pull over, cursing the day he took this job and threaten to tell our parents. But the poor man, who was still driving the bus when we graduated, got a few minutes' break every day when the bus arrived at the top of the road leading to the city. The sea would suddenly appear before the eyes of those loud village kids who were used to rivers and bumpy roads, and like magic, it would cast them into complete silence. We would sit glued to our windows, gazing with awe at the two ships docked alone amidst all that blue, there in the Mediterranean. Observing that painting of the morning sea was the only real moment of happiness in a day where lessons and sermons and homework competed for our time, and the idea of sailing would wipe out, if only for a while, the melancholy of reading books with no pictures and of the cold rooms that awaited us, filled only with the faces of teachers who never smiled.

During the day, I feel a strong need to be able to see the distant harbor from my room, but at night its faint flickering lights are enough to assure me that someone is working when I go to sleep.

This evening I also moved the comfortable couch to the living room; I used to lie down on it and cuddle up whenever I had a hard time coming up with images. When my mother asked me why I moved the couch out of my room, I told her that I didn't want this room any more and that she could knock the wall down and have the bigger guest room she has always wanted. My sudden willingness to let go surprised my sister, who said she thought I had changed lately and didn't like it. I asked her what she meant, and she said she had noticed me sitting and looking out into the void, thinking, that I had not been doing anything, not reading or writing, or going out with friends. And she added that this change worried her; she didn't know why, "Maybe because I'm used to you being different."

I returned to the room and took down the only painting decorating the walls. I decided to destroy it. I wouldn't take it back to its owner, nor to give it away as a gift. I'd destroy it. It was called *The Call of the Sea*—I don't know why; there was no sea in it, not even water. The painter called it *The Call of the Sea,* and although the name wasn't inscribed on it anywhere, this name became part of it. Whenever I looked at it (and I looked at it and thought about it unintentionally more than ten times a day) I was aware that I was looking at *The Call of the Sea*. A small forest, a red horizon, some men and a woman, tame animals, and small things that are hard to describe. When I came back from college, I found an icon of the Virgin Mary and Baby Jesus and a picture of my grandfather with his traditional outfit, his full armor, and his soft complexion, hanging on the walls of the room that had been my father's during the short time he'd gotten to live in this house. At first I left these things up and added the movie poster of *Orchestra Rehearsal,* which Lutfi had given me. Then I took them all down and put up *The Call of the Sea* all by itself. And today I decided to destroy it. I waited until my mother and sister went to bed. I got a knife from the kitchen and slashed the painting; then I went outside and threw it into the dumpster, hoping the garbage truck would come by tomorrow morning and pick it up.

I came back and wrote everything down in Lara's notebook. The moon is out tonight. From time to time, I can hear machine gun fire and see light streak the sky in the distance. The phone is ringing at this late hour. For a moment I think it might be Lara calling from New York. I hurry to pick up the phone. No one. Tonight, I'll sleep well.

Friday, June 26, 1986

Today, I woke up thinking of Uncle Rafael although nothing has happened recently to remind me of him. I think I saw him in a dream—one of those deep dreams that disappear completely when I wake up. I barely remember any of my dreams. The last one was vivid and detailed. We were on the hill covered with olive trees, Mary and I, on the hill where the ancient brick house

29

stands on its own. We used to go there on holidays when we were young to play with the monkey in the cage, or fight with the parrot, or feed the peacock and the turkeys, until the lady who owned the house threw stones at us from her balcony and we hid behind the trees nearby. We, Mary and I, were on top of the same hill, but it was bare, with no trace of the olive trees. The ancient brick house wasn't there either. On the hilltop, there were only two tall cypress trees embracing each other and blowing in the breeze. It was sunset, and we were sitting on two fancy, plush chairs, almost like the thrones used in plays by kings and queens. We enjoyed the scene of the glowing horizon; everything was in its full beauty until the old lady who owned the house came up to us and said that our time was up and that we had to leave because it was someone else's turn to watch the sun set. The idea of the sun actually setting was absent from the dream, but it was as if the red sun was permanently in the process of sinking into the far horizon of the sea.

I had this dream about a week ago, and I can't forget it. But today, I woke up thinking of Uncle Rafael. My mother visits him almost every day. I haven't seen him in months. I got into the habit of not visiting my maternal grandfather's house when I was a kid, because they lived in another neighborhood, and I still don't, even now that the problems between the neighborhoods are over. Anyway, Uncle Rafael rarely stayed at home in his youth. Now, that he's moved to this house—the house he doesn't leave and where he wears a wool hat that covers his ears in winter, I actually don't try to see him anymore. It's hard to explain, but somehow Uncle Rafael's story constantly buzzes in my head.

Yesterday, when my sister asked me about *The Call of the Sea,* I told her I gave it to one of my friends. She was surprised because she hadn't seen me take it out of the house. Then she said the walls in the room looked bare now, so I told her that's how I liked them to look. She smiled, unconvinced.

Sunday, June 28, 1986

Uncle Mansour came to visit us today. He came early to be sure he'd find me at home, or so he said. I was still in bed. My mother, clearly looking worried, accompanied him to my bedroom. She closed the door and left; then he sat next to me on the bed. He started the conversation by saying, "Ever since my brother died, I only come to this house to see you," and pointing behind him, he added, "I don't worry about the women; they are capable of managing the toughest situations." I laughed remembering that, one day, Uncle Mansour suddenly stopped talking to his wife and two daughters and didn't say a single word to either one of them for several years.

He is the eldest, and his brothers appointed him as the signal man—that is, someone like a harbor master who directs ships at a port—after he got shot in the foot under circumstances that had nothing to do with our "family incidents," circumstances he never wished to talk about. One of his first duties to the other brothers was to never get in trouble with the law and never do anything that resulted in his being held for investigation. As he was the one who set the time for ambushes and attacks, he had to be in public places while the attacks were being carried out in order to ensure himself a number of disinterested alibis. My uncle was his brothers' eyes, because when someone is running from the authorities, he's like a blind man who needs someone to lead him. Uncle Mansour picked a hiding place for each one of them and made sure that none of them knew where the other was hiding. If warned that the hiding place was no longer a secret, he ordered them to move. He provided food and cigarettes, bought witnesses, and paid bribes, even to the police officers. He said that if one of us died, it was from not following his advice to the letter.

Years of doing this have caused his head to sink between his shoulders, and he still walks in the shade of the wall, sits with a wall behind him, and peeks out of his back door if the front bell rings—he has never, by the way, lived in a house with only one door. He doesn't speak to two people at the same time and generally prefers signals to speech.

Caution has taken root in all of us to the extent that, during the years I spent in Syracuse, it was amazing how I, instinctively, chose a room that didn't overlook the street, how I avoided all kinds of crowds, and how I always sat next to the wall in study halls or cafés.

Uncle Mansour isn't just afraid of outright dangers or uncertain situations. He's afraid of people, too— or people especially. He's experienced so many kinds of evil and betrayal that he's now suspicious of nuns, do-gooders, doctors, and friends excited about friendship. He only visits us when he's worried about our safety, my safety, really. He arrives, stands at the door, and asks his question. My mother gives him a hesitant answer that he's usually not satisfied with. He makes a rattling sound and shakes his head. Then he pulls his shirt away from his chest with two fingers and brushes it off. He turns and walks away while his eyes, hands, and shoulders still say, "Don't say I didn't warn you. I'm not responsible for what happens next." He used to keep up with the small-est details of my life. He would ask my mother, "What's the boy doing in his room all the time?" And if she told him I was reading or writing, he would produce the same series of signs and leave. I sometimes think that since we've laid down our arms and made peace with our enemies, Uncle Mansour lives only to prove his suspicions that life is a series of ambushes. I don't think he's totally wrong about that.

And he even came here today to warn me again of a possible threat. But he preferred first to encourage me to get married. He had been informed that I was seeing someone and he preferred someone who could "put up" with me. I interrupted him to ask what he meant by what he said on the phone, and I told him that it worried my mother. He said he was sure something was going to happen and that we should be careful since we've already paid a huge price. I asked him whether my aunt knew about it, but he said he rarely saw my aunt, and that never in his life had he confided in a woman, not even my grandmother. After that, he urged me to find a job, reminding me how my father had sweated and toiled to buy this property for us and saying it would be shameful for a man to have to sell his land or house in order to pay his bills.

When he left, I hurried to comfort my mother and tell her that Uncle Mansour was just imagining the dangers he mentioned and that we shouldn't worry about his words of warning.

In the evening, I watched the eight o'clock news

with my mother and sister. They were happy and surprised that I was sitting with them in the living room. Since I stopped writing and shuffled the furniture around in my bedroom, I've been trying to avoid being alone by leaving my bedroom door open all the time. From now on, I don't think I will be able to sit and meditate about what is happening to me. I can't tolerate examining and reexamining what I've done anymore. I count myself among the cowards who do not look life in the face and who do not try to hold onto life with their bare hands.

Tuesday, June 30, 1986

Today was a day of truce. A day of balance and calmness, as if I were starting to get used to my new lifestyle. I talked on the phone with Mary. She said that I sounded different, that I was speaking slowly and seriously.

I must finish what I started and return to the resolutions I wrote down in red ink in my address book. Tomorrow, I will start with the meals.

Wednesday, July 1, 1986

I succeeded in convincing my mother and sister that we should all have lunch together, at the dining table, at a specific time. I suggested one o'clock sharp. They both said they were always at home anyway, and all I had to do was be there any time I chose. We usually eat in the kitchen, separately, whenever we're hungry. I hardly ever see my mother eating. I think my father was the cause of this lack of structure because he never ate lunch before three in the afternoon. I'll go one extra step every day. They both enjoy my company and will be cooperative. Today my mother objected to the idea at first, saying she hadn't eaten like this, ever; my sister said she would be very embarrassed if anyone came in and found us sitting, the three of us alone, eating slowly and politely; all that was missing were the lighted candles.

Tomorrow, we will start having lunch at the dining table.

Saturday, July 4, 1986

Instead of going to the café in Al-Midan Square, I found myself lost this morning, drifting around in our old neighborhood, around the house that still stands there, faded as its colors were, between the church and St. Joseph's School on one side and the river road on the other. I got there on foot, seeking to discover the secret power of these places because now, whenever I hear— just as when I was in the States—that people had deserted a village during the war or that its enemies destroyed it, I blame the village. If it hadn't been founded so feebly and hastily in the first place, it wouldn't vanish like that. The fact that its people accept the idea of leaving their homes and of going on with their lives, remaining healthy, working and plodding along, only proves that homelessness is inherent in them. So I blame it on them, too. I have no fear, for example, that this would ever happen to us. Not because we have no enemies or because our enemies are weak, but because our places—the houses built so close together, pulsing with life, the classroom my mother studied in at St. Joseph's School, the orange groves surrounded by curtains of sugarcane—have enough tenacity and resistance to keep them going forever. I walked down today to see with my own eyes just what material this resistance is made of.

I walk down to our old neighborhood every once in a while; my heart misses these damp side streets that wake up early in the morning to a long spring, and I miss the old church; I'll never give up the idea that, after I die, I'll keep close to the church, under the quinine trees, near the people walking by, the car horns, and the mothers calling their mischievous boys. When I wander around here for about an hour, aimlessly, slowly, and sip water from the fountain where the brand name "Pont à Mousson" is engraved, or when one of our old neighbors recognizes me and asks me about my mother—

"How's she doing?" "Oh, fine," I say, and she answers "Thank goodness,"—then my soul regains some of its strength.

Today I wandered all the way down to the road leading to the orange groves. I wanted to retrace the route of our family picnic, the only project, besides taking care of life's basic necessities, that my father organized. My father was usually harried for time and busy with his work, but once or twice a year, he would suddenly stop everything. He'd leave very early as usual, frowning and content, but then he'd come back and yell, "To the river!" We'd get into the car, my grandmother in the front seat next to my dad, my mother and we children in the back. Nevertheless, no sign of vacation or happiness would show on his face or change his manners. Just as stern as usual, he'd drive us, take out the stuff from the car at the shady spot on the river bank, arrange the place, line up the kababs on the skewer, crush the garlic, grill the meat, and fan the flames while we ran around, here and there. He usually did half the work alone, while my mother smiled and nudged us to look at him, the man who usually asked to have his shoes brought to him at home and who knew nothing but how to give orders. Toward noon, everything would be ready, and he would call out loud again, "Time to eat!" Then, when he sat down with us in the circle, the glass of arrack diluted with cold water in front of him—only then did he take a deep breath, and his face relaxed. He'd ask my mother to sing—we'd be eating and my dad drinking. He admired her voice and used to accompany her a little with his gruff voice. That was his happy day—he would have decided to make it happen and enjoy it with us and our grandmother. He would look at my sister and me and laugh, and then, as if his eyes had gotten lost somewhere far away, his laugh would freeze for a moment and then resume.

Today, I insisted on us all sitting down and getting up from the table at the same time, and I explained that there was no reason for my mother and my sister to go back and forth between the dining room and the kitchen: they could put everything on the table before we sat down, including fruits. I felt they were more responsive to me today, and they were both smiling as they set the table; my mother even wanted to take out the fancy set of china she keeps with the other personal belongings she brought with her when she got married. I told her there's no need to get out those plates because we'll always be eating like this. Next week, I will start negotiating with them about supper.

Monday, July 6, 1986

I woke up thinking of my Uncle Rafael again. I asked my mother about him and she said, "Nothing new." I often remember what my grandmother once said when I was ten or maybe younger, "The boy has something of his uncle Rafael." Her words carried a certain fear as well as a thinly disguised sarcasm. I still don't know what that something is that I've inherited from Uncle Rafael. I know his whole story—my mother has told it to me over and over, and she gets teary-eyed every time. Why does it scare me, why don't I take his story the way I know it and write it down, get it all out and be free of it? Oh God, how is this going to end; how shall I be saved from writing?

My mother says he was born with his two front teeth, fully grown, next to each other. The news spread, and people in the neighborhood were worried something really bad might happen, and since it was very hot, they were sure it was going to be an earthquake. As for the red stamp in the center of his forehead, they had an explanation for that: my grandmother said that she had craved unripe dates when she was pregnant, and that the pregnancy had been difficult.

When he was four, he got a fever, and no one knew what from—here my mother's eyes get teary—so they soaked him in mint and oil and read some prayers over him, but to no use. They melted lead over fire and poured it into water, and their neighbor Saada's face appeared at the bottom of the pot. They sent someone to secretly tear a piece of her dress to burn, and they burned it like incense over him. They tied a bundle of the twigs of the cross and a blue bead around his waist, but it didn't help. Finally they made a vow to the Virgin Mary that he would wear her celestial red and blue dress for a whole year and he was cured.

Then when he was eight, they sent him to a boarding school, but the very first term, he came up with a arrangement that made everyone happy and which lasted throughout his stay there: he would spend two years in each class, after which the principal would promote him no matter what his report card said. His report card was almost blank except for his grades in math, where he showed such genius that his teachers had to shut him up so he wouldn't anticipate solutions to problems the other kids were solving on the board. During his stay there, he used to do all sorts of favors for the school. He helped at mass every morning and led the children's chorus; then he specialized in repairing furniture and lavatories, and painting the wooden seats. He also joined the band where he excelled in all the wind instruments, especially those that required long breaths—his huge body and broad chest helping him with that—and he devoted himself to lifting heavy weights and took on the job of carrying the old invalid Arabic philosophy teacher up to the second floor every day and then back down when the lesson was over.

During one of the summer breaks, my grandfather

took him by the hand and led him to the courthouse in town. The clerk, who was standing right next to him, called my uncle's name very loudly and that startled him. The transcriber sat him on a chair with a table in front of it, like the tables at school, and my grandfather started explaining the following reasons for the appeal:

"In my youth, I traveled to Venezuela, where I spent about eight years making a living in all sorts of trades. All my work was crowned with success that exceeded my expectations, and I managed to save up a large sum of money, but I was constantly yearning to come back to my homeland and my family. I was satisfied with what God had blessed me with to that point, closed out my business, and came back to my country with a big picture of Venezuela's liberator, Simon Bolivar, in a golden frame. It still hangs in my house in the middle of my living room.

"While on board the ship that was carrying me home, I made a vow that if I got married and if God blessed me with sons, I would give the oldest the name of this hero, as a tribute from me to Venezuela and its people. And that's what happened. I got married and started a household, but when my wife had our oldest son, a young bachelor brother of mine had passed away in a painful accident, and I had to name my first son after my brother. After God blessed us with two daughters, we had this son and I said to myself, it's time to fulfill my promise, and I named my boy Bolivar. I was glad he was a handsome boy, strongly built, and deserving of his name. But as he grew up and mixed with his friends and went to school, I discovered that I'd done him wrong and given him a burden he couldn't bear. Because he is, your Honor, extremely docile; he doesn't pay much heed to strength and courage, unlike his brother who isn't afraid of fighting or of challenges. Every time I look at him, I become more convinced of the saying, 'Life is a garden with different flowers.' This is how his name has become a cause for ridicule to him, and to me, and to the 'Liberatador.' That is why I'm appealing to you to relieve him of the name Bolivar, and to call him Rafael, thus allowing me to place him under the protection of one of the angels standing at the doors of Heaven, because he is, I believe, in dire need of this protection."

Good luck had it that the judge wasn't too busy with other appointments that day, and he was a man of literature and eloquence, versed in the Bible, especially the Old Testament. So he responded to my grandfather's plea, trying to convince him to give up his idea, reminding him of the responsibility the name Rafael throws on its bearer—for he was the one who healed Tobias from his blindness and saved his son from the whale and his wife from Satan. The two men had a long discussion, during which the subject of all the discussion was tired and fell asleep. The judge turned around and saw him smiling in his sleep, his head leaning on his hand, so he hurried to end the procedures, addressing the transcriber, "Issue a ruling to allow this boy's name to be changed."

Then he turned to my grandfather and said, "You must pay the fee as well as the cost to announce the name change in the official newspaper."

Uncle Rafael left school at age fifteen and woke up at twenty. He parted his hair down the middle, let his handkerchief show out of the pocket of his suit coat and set out. At the beginning he would leave in the morning and come back at sunset; then his trips became longer till he got his parents used to not waiting for him to come back. He would often pack a small suitcase with nightclothes, throw a coat on his arm on cold days, and walk away. He would leave clean and fresh and come back withered. And if he ever spent a whole day at home, it would only be to bathe, polish his shoes and shine them, and iron his shirts and ties himself.

He'd disappear, and we'd hear rumors about his whereabouts. One person said he was at the capital at one of those old and tattered hotels whose back windows overlook the market, sharing his room with a short man who had freckles and who was a professional gambler. And another saw him—his suit coat with a red carnation—taking a cab with a violinist and an oud player to an unknown destination. And someone said he lived in an apartment in one of the nearby suburbs with two sisters, one a spinster who took care of the housework and prepared hot meals, and the other, deserted by her husband, who put make-up on every morning and spent the rest of the day in bed in her night gown. They were letting him stay there, or rather, renting a room for him and giving him the key. Or we'd hear that every Monday and Thursday Rafael was going to the church in one of the nearby villages and took part in their feet washing ceremony; he volunteered to be Judas Iscariot, and when the ceremony was over, he would sneak out the back door of the church, and the faithful would follow him into the alleyways with curses, stones, and rotten fruits. He'd raise his suit collar over his ears and run.

When any of his family confronted him with these stories, he'd only laugh and try to change the subject. But he'd always try to comfort them: if he stayed away too long and couldn't report he was okay, he'd send a message on the radio during "Listeners' Requests"—a message accompanied by a song to tell them how much he had missed them.

When my grandfather passed away unexpectedly, (when he lost his footing and fell), they sent someone to track down Uncle Rafael. For a whole day he traveled from one of Uncle Rafael's known burrows to the next, looking for him in vain. Finally, at sunset, they asked for him and found him in the middle of an olive grove in one of the Bedouin camps, sitting in a wicker chair, well dressed and his hair glossy, among a gathering of women wrapped in shawls and barefoot children who were screaming around him and fighting in the mud. He was sitting there, his right sleeve rolled up, while a sharp-looking Bedouin with green eyes and dark skin drew a tattoo on his arm.

They came back with Uncle Rafael after the funeral, and he cried for hours; then he fell into a kind of stupor. He spent three days sitting in the center of the reception hall, next to my Uncle Ibrahim, accepting condolences under the portrait of Simon Bolivar, wiping the sweat off his forehead and face with a handkerchief, his face divided between fear and doubt. Every once in a while, he let out a long sigh that put a stop to all the gossip going around, reminding the people of the occasion they were gathered for. Some people would start feeling a little sleepy in that silence, which was interrupted only by the noise of the waiter as he served coffee to the circle of people with his brass pot.

My mother remembers that period very well and tells of how Uncle Rafael stayed home after the people left. He would wake up early, attire himself to perfection, sit alone in the reception room, and let out his long sigh that rippled through the quiet house. At noon he sat at the table, ate politely, kissed my grandmother's hand, thanked my mother, and went back to his seat. He'd crane his neck every time he heard a noise, examine the few visitors suspiciously and cautiously, then sink back into silence to jump with fear if my grandmother called him from the kitchen. At night we heard his soft and continuous moans that mixed harmoniously with the crickets under the full moon and the backward barking of the neighbors' senile dog.

He stayed in that condition until the mass of the fortieth day. Then he packed his suitcase and placed it on a chair next to the door. He went to church with his family and relatives, sat in the front row, listened attentively with his head down, and shook his head the whole time until the priest got to the section of the Bible where Christ said, "Stay awake, because you know not when the thief might come and find you asleep." In his rough high voice, Uncle Rafael took part in chanting the Syriac hymns he knew by heart. When mass was over, he put a large sum of money at the altar, went back to the house, didn't go in, stood at the door, carried his suitcase and walked away.

What people didn't say about him, the mail took care of. No more than a week would go by before mail was waiting for him at the house, his only permanent address: a bundle of letters including the journal *Popular Poetry,* to which he had a continuous subscription, in addition to a torrent of invitations to weddings and funerals, in the south and the east of the country. My mother kept them all in a drawer, and she didn't mind opening a few and laughing as she read them. Among these letters were some with women's perfume or some imprinted with a lipstick kiss. Or that telegraph with one short question in Egyptian dialect, "Why are you doing this to me?" signed, *Afaf.* The drawer filled up with photographs as the days went by, and my mother, as well as my aunt, had a good time looking at them.

News about him was abundant and conflicting. It was falsely said he had won the jackpot of the Labor Day lottery, and had asked to remain anonymous. Then it was said that he was selling blessings from the Pope, hand-signed by His Holiness, and also honorary diplomas from remote universities. And it was said that he was doing an archeological search when he found the head of a Roman Caesar and that the government was after him.

Then suddenly he came back. It happened on Ash Wednesday. He had gone to church in the morning where the priest drew a cross with ashes over the red birthmark still in the center of his forehead. A cab was waiting for him at the door, and he urged the driver to leave quickly because he was late for an appointment.

But at seven that same evening, he knocked at the door. He had the key in his pocket, but he preferred to knock on the door with his fist. My aunt opened it for him— my mother had gotten married and left her parents' house, but she, too, has tears when she tells how the ashes were still stuck to his forehead. He was not forty yet. His hair had started thinning, and some white had sneaked its way to his sideburns, but he was still lively and fresh. He leaned against the doorway and dropped his suitcase. He was casting a new look at his surroundings, the look of someone who had just discovered a big secret and was reevaluating long-gone things. He stared at his sister's face as if seeing it for the first time. He looked at Simon Bolivar, asked about my grandmother, kissed her on the head and sat down. He spent the next day sitting on the balcony, in a rocking chair, with the same astonishment in his eyes. A few days later, his looks were more stable, but he didn't leave the balcony. Every morning he waited for the wandering newspaper boy who called the news from the top of the street and was accompanied by the neighbors' dog. He'd signal to him and buy the news-paper. He would put it in his coat pocket, then go back to his chair on the balcony, watching the boy walk away and the dog pant after him till they disappeared in the dusty street. He'd wrap himself in a big *abaya,* and on cold days he'd make sure to cover his head with a leather hat lined with wool that hung over his ears in a funny way; only rarely would he do away with the hat.

Oh. Now I have written it down; maybe I won't have to worry about it anymore. I've written it down the way my mother tells it and repeats it. Every time I hear her talk about her brother Rafael, I wonder about the sadness that falls over her, because I have only known my uncle in his good "flashes," when he used to visit us in a hurry and hug us to his chest a little and I used to smell his cologne—my uncle was the only man I knew who wore cologne—then he used to sneak some small notes into my hand and a handful of sugar-coated nuts. Considering my uncles on my father's side, who are always frowning, and my father whose days were stitched from a cluster of duties that couldn't be postponed or taken lightly, Uncle Rafael was the holidays' only oasis— he had something feminine about him, and life spread out from his palms then into a wide open space, interrupted only by uncertain duties and organized by laws he voluntarily imposed. My mother still cries when she tells us anecdotes about him.

Wednesday, July 8, 1986

Yesterday, I sent Lara a postcard through the same travel agency, so I don't know if she's going to get it. I only wrote four lines on the back of the card, "I just want to know if you've been getting my letters. I just want to be sure that you're still out there, somewhere between New York and Greece, and that you still care to hear about me. I'm on my way to becoming a different person."

In the nearby vacant lot, the children of our neighborhood are practicing throwing boomerangs. We have many emigrants in Australia; one of them must have sent these boomerangs. The children scream louder whenever the piece of wood comes close to the person who threw it.

Friday, July 10, 1986

All the books cramming up the closet are beginning to be a real problem. I haven't been reading much since I stopped writing and reflecting, it's true, but I also need to break the spell because I've decided to take up the fight face to face, and the books are standing in my way. What should I do with them? The closet which I cram my books into, two rows deep, was originally a wardrobe. I bought it from an antique dealer who insisted on making me listen to his theory of the imminent collapse of some nations and the ultimate victory of socialism. When I bought the wardrobe, I was, and still am, fond of using things in ways different than the way they're meant to be used. It took a lot of effort, but we moved it to the garden, and I started cleaning it. Slogans and drawings were scribbled all over it, including a picture of a young woman running her fingers through her hair. The wardrobe had three mirrors, one on each door; so I removed two and replaced them with transparent glass, keeping the big mirror in the middle—the one that reflected a part of the city's harbor when I sat at my table to write. I bought this closet immediately after I graduated and came back from the United States, and it was soon crammed with books on different subjects and in different languages. I was afflicted with the buying virus for a whole two years. I had a passion for Canaanite mythology, detective stories, Islamic jurisprudence, and modern European poetry, all at the same time, and it even got to a point where I sometimes bought novels in Portuguese, along with Wittgenstein's *Tractatus* in German, although I couldn't read a word of either language.

I remember how my sister ridiculed and resented me at the time, but she doesn't know that I'll soon start getting rid of these books just as I got rid of *The Call of the Sea*. What she also doesn't know is that I have to finish my project before the autumn equinox arrives when the orange glow is only a harbinger of the end, and my willpower dissolves, and I become weak and unable to act or make any decisions. Anyway, I think that my mother and sister have been whispering about my change in behavior and have been hoping to marry me off as soon as possible.

Sunday, July 12, 1986

Mary came by this Sunday. We drove around as usual and ducked into side roads and hugged and kissed for a long time. We don't talk much anymore. When we meet, we find ourselves waiting to be alone again. I tried to break this cycle today and told her about the dream I had where we were watching the sunset together, and I pointed toward the hill covered with olive trees and the brick house that still stands alone on top of it. But again, I couldn't get her to talk, and we sank back in kisses and sighs. Before she left, she said I was beginning to scare her; I didn't ask her what she meant because I understood. She doesn't feel safe with me anymore, and she is justified in feeling that way.

Thursday, July 16, 1986

Today, after lunch I sat next to my sister on the balcony where she usually works on her embroidery and listens to the "Radio Love Station." I wanted us to have a conversation so that she would feel I am myself still, the brother she knows. So, I started to entertain her with stories, and she told me she heard that Brother Shafiq had fallen out with a group of his followers who had analyzed the numerical value of the letters of his name in Syriac in accordance with the Book of Revelation and discovered that he is among the false prophets. It all started when he claimed that the Virgin Mary was going to meet him in Ain Jawz, and he took his followers with him to the village where they slept out in the open for four damp nights in a row, and when Virgin Mary did not appear, and they asked him what they were doing there, he accused them of having little faith. So they argued, and it seems that our friend Lutfi was one of the people who broke away from Brother Shafiq's group.

As we talked, we watched the few people who passed by on the street. Soon, Lutfi walked by. It was four o'clock, and he was on his way to the movie theater. My sister asked me to call him so we could ask him about Brother Shafiq's group—I think my sister has a crush on Lutfi. When I called him, he apologized because he was late for work. We know this movie theater well, and we know all the stories about it from Lutfi. My sister now knows the frequent moviegoers one by one and can count them on her fingers because she watches them every day, at exactly four o'clock, pushing through the door of Cinéma Royale. Every day, because Najib Al-Bahri, the owner of the movie theater, for cheap prices has been renting movies that are not much in demand. He shows them every day, saving action movies and love and passion movies for Sunday and the holidays.

The first visitor in the theater is Rabi; he never misses a day, maybe because he gets in for free, being a relative of Najib Al-Bahri's wife. He's an overgrown young boy, roaming the streets all day, eating candy and barking like a dog. He ends up near the movie theater an hour before the door is open, an hour which he spends looking at the theater announcements and posters, pointing them out to the passersby, chomping on a big apple and laughing. When he first started coming to Cinéma Royale, Rabi started clapping his thick hands whenever he thought the scene called for applause, whenever he saw a kiss or a fight. He made the audience so angry that Al-Bahri threatened to throw him out, and he settled for clapping only twice, once at the beginning and once at the end of the movie.

Two sisters usually come after Rabi and sit in the back seat on the right. They are followed by two young men who smoke and look sideways at the girls until the lights are turned off and they exchange places, one of the guys moving to sit next to his girlfriend and her sister moving to sit next to his buddy. They whisper and hold hands throughout the movie and keep looking left and right before stealing a shy hot kiss in the dark—until the moment the music gets louder signaling that the movie is about to end, and they go back to their original seats before the theater lights expose them.

As for Mr. Anees, the schoolteacher, he always comes in jogging as if he were late. He has been a regular visitor for a long time, since the fifties, when they started showing the American World War II movies. The subject concerns him personally. After all, hadn't he been arrested by French officers in 1944 and charged with belonging to the Nazi party and transmitting information over the wireless? The people of the village knew that he had bought a very expensive radio only to listen to the Arabic Berlin Broadcasting Station. Later Mr. Anees kept explaining to his students that the war wasn't over and that Hitler was still alive and was sure to come back. The veteran moviegoers of Cinéma Royale remember how he used to shout, protesting scenes about the destruction of Nuremberg. When he dozed off, there was always someone who poked him and then his voice mingled with whistling from the audience, forcing Al-Bahri to turn the lights on and calm him down several times. He gradually gave in and is now content with mumbling;

only those sitting next to him can hear, and they smile. But he's never missed a movie except in the case of sickness or emergency, and he has been sitting in the same seat on the right side next to the wall, taking off his hat and placing it on his lap, wearing his glasses, and watching attentively like someone reading a book written in very fine print.

There is also Moussa who cannot read the Arabic subtitles and is always asking his neighbors what's happening on the screen, a habit which has made his friends stop coming to the movies altogether. The truth is he has gotten much better; he is not the way he used to be when he first started coming—like a deaf man at a symphony—with time, he has developed the ability, not to read, but to get the general idea of what's going on. When he gets mixed up, he relies on the postman, who tries to sit a few rows away from him.

As for Aziz, he is a rookie moviegoer who has been coming for almost a year now, ever since his daughter got married and he couldn't persuade his new son-in-law, Saeed, that the newlyweds should come to live with him. Having been left to face his wife alone at home, Aziz has been escaping to Cinéma Royale. He comes to the matinée every day, greets Najib Al-Bahri and heads for the front row, two meters away from the screen, where he plops down on the first seat. He follows the first few scenes, then closes his eyes and falls into a deep sleep, and only the lights and the commotion of the people leaving awaken him from it. Sometimes he sleeps even through this, and when Lutfi has to shake him by the shoulder, he wakes up disoriented and asks what time it is.

I am one of Cinéma Royale's best customers, too. I've never stopped going. It's right across the street, an extension of our house. But I'm different from the others because all those people I mix with inside the dark theater, those my sister counts every day from our balcony as they hurry in, in order not to miss the beginning of the movie, all those people are strong, or so I imagine at least. They're stronger than the movies: after the show they go out into the light of the street and in one brief moment return to what they had been. Isadora Duncan returns to the movie reel boxes in Lutfi's cold storeroom, and the "singer but not the song" also returns. Mr. Anees, Moussa, and the others have their own lives, which no one can penetrate, whereas I'm wide open, useless; I watched *The Great Gatsby* once, and it haunted me for a decade.

I will fortify myself even against the movies.

Thursday, July 23, 1986

This afternoon, my aunt sent a messenger saying that my grandmother wanted to see us, my sister and me. That was enough to make us realize that my grandmother, who has been crippled by her illness for a year, is approaching her end. Her turn has come—my grandmother, who is a lot like a man and who used to say whenever the church bell rang mournfully, "Women are happy now because whores love to cry." Of course, whenever the bell rang mournfully, she'd be afraid it was ringing for one of her relatives. My mother went with us, although the girl my aunt had sent didn't mention her.

My grandmother's head was propped up on two pillows. I kissed her on the cheek, and she whispered that I should take care of myself and kissed my sister and my mother and spoke in a low voice. I went back home, alone. In the evening, when my mother and sister returned, they told me, laughing, that my grandmother had forgotten to ask me to take care of the pomegranate tree, and when she remembered in the afternoon, she asked my aunt to tell me to take care of it. They also told me that, at around four o'clock, she sat up in her bed and looked comfortable; she asked for my uncle and told her son and daughter she didn't want to have the archbishop say her burial prayers, but would rather have the village priests, especially Father Antoun. Then she urged my aunt to get out the bed sheets my grandmother had kept new and clean especially for this day. She even allocated the different kitchen chores to the women. Why was this woman entering darkness with her eyes open? If I told Lara about my grandmother, she wouldn't believe me.

When I came back, I found Nirmal standing in our garden, next to the roses, smiling and looking toward the street to where the Fine Arts students had stood. My arrival surprised him: he was embarrassed, and laughing loudly, he said in his broken English that our garden reminds him of his father's in Punjab. He added that he was standing there because he was sure that his family is gathered in their garden at this hour, too, talking about him, reading his last letter, and laughing.

Monday, July 27, 1986

Friday evening, my grandmother passed away. I sat for three days next to my uncles, their sons, and our relatives, receiving condolences. This ancestry elated me, this feeling of power at seeing all these strong men unified. I was relieved to look at these silent family members who were not faking sadness or putting on frowns over the death of this tough woman who lived every day of her life to the fullest because they know the other pain, the pain of years harvested in their prime. I have experienced this pain: seeing my cousin carried up on the men's shoulders, a young man, wearing a pink shirt, his chest torn apart by bullets. Today, I couldn't remember the faces of the men who had carried him without a coffin up the stairs when I was five years old. I don't know how I got there; they combed my hair and sat me beside him while he lay on his white iron bed, and the women clutched different pieces of clothing he had worn. My grandmother entered—my same grandmother who planted the pomegranate tree for me. She stood in the doorway, leaning on her stick and screamed at the women, "Shut up," then sat down and kissed my cousin's hands without crying. My grandmother never cried; nobody made her cry except my aunt who, when they carried the corpse out of the house, released two stinging screams that were not suitable for someone of my grandmother's age.

In church I tried to re-experience the joy that I have when the Syriac hymns start, two groups of priests to either side of the altar singing them. I shiver and enjoy the singing just the way I enjoy, in the solitude of my room, my mother's voice form the kitchen, singing what she says was a popular love song from Baghdad that starts with, "Ahmad Muhammad Ali Pasha, my death he wanted. . . ."

After the funeral, my uncles and relatives began whispering; one of them was seriously concerned about what his neighbor was confiding to him. Then they withdrew to the balcony or to the inside rooms. Uncle Mansour was the most vibrant. He bent over me and whispered something in my ear, and I pretended I understood and nodded my head several times so he wouldn't raise his voice to make me hear. Why is it always a state of emergency in our family, although the wound has already scarred over, as my mother says, and reconciliation has taken place—this reconciliation they described to me more than once because I was in the States when it happened: they described how those men were reconciled when they didn't know each other and how they exchanged toasts during the dinner that brought them together and then exchanged visits like intimate friends for two months or more. Afterwards, the relationships between them became cold, the visits stopped, and they would meet in the streets and not shake hands, but only wave from a distance—a gesture between being cold and ignoring the other person.

My relatives were whispering while I sat down seriously. For three days, I didn't leave my spot; I hardly spoke to anyone, even when we gathered around the lunch table to eat in that horrific way I cannot stand anymore. They were whispering and discussing unimportant issues. I was studying the way I sat, keeping my body from slouching by stretching my back and legs, and I stayed in this rigid, tiring position for nearly an hour, clasping my hands at my stomach or resting them over my thighs, my head turned away from my body, and looking into the distance. That's how I've spent the time trying to find the perfect way to sit, one which would gather me around myself to be tenacious, alert, and handsome. I continued to work on it at home, taking advantage of my mother's and sister's absence at my grandmother's funeral. I placed a chair in front of the wardrobe's mirror and started shifting around again till I came close to a position that I thought suited me and my new image of myself. Perhaps I was still missing a cane or an umbrella in winter to add to my poise and my self-confidence.

On Saturday, after the funeral, Uncle Rafael came to offer condolences. As soon as he came in with his flabby fat body, everybody started whispering. Uncle Rafael is famous for the stories about him, and he rarely leaves his house. He sat next to me, then leaned over and said he misses seeing me and hearing me talk about the books I've been reading about the country's political situation. He reeked of garlic. I remembered my mother telling us that Uncle Rafael ate garlic on an empty stomach in the morning because it reduces the risk of heart diseases. He got that advice from one of his friends, the "wise" Bedouins. My grandmother passed away before I dared ask her what it is that's so similar between Uncle Rafael and me—not that I want to deny this similarity. I just want to put my finger on it. I want to understand how my uncle with his bloated body, how this man who is happy, content, and always smiling, could be like me, so downcast and lonely all the time that I can't stand it and that it leads me to fall into my present predicament.

Thursday, July 30, 1986

I spent yesterday afternoon trying to classify my books. First I set aside the detective novels because they don't leave any room for secrets, and then the modern poetry books because they make a religion out of a secret. I packed these two kinds into a box, and this morning I donated them to the public library where most of the holdings go back to the days of the traveling "JFK Library." The librarian half-smiled when she saw Agatha Christie's and Dashiell Hammett's books, raised her eyebrows in surprise at the poetry anthologies like *The Circular State of Madness,* and burst out laughing when she got to *The Moon Shepherd Looking at Himself in the Water.*

I had no difficulty getting rid of the detective novels because I had never felt the need to hold onto those small yellow and black books after I read them, their pages faded and wilted, kind of like milk with the cream skimmed off, stories that rush headlong toward their endings without stopping for the sake of curiosity to consider some scene off the main road. What gets to me the most about these stories is that they don't forget anyone and do not quit until they send all the characters to their final fates—death or death's sister, "happily ever after." I have devoured dozens of those tales, if not hundreds, each time trying to recapture a certain pleasure from childhood when we, my sister and I, used to pair up and lean playing cards against each other, and spend almost half an hour trying to make them stand, one behind the other on the floor of the guest room, only to destroy, in one second, what we had built. We would tap the last cards with one finger and watch the whole long line collapse in a single move while we screamed out in delight. That's the detective novel—no sooner do I read its still words on the page than they fall flat on the ground, as if once was all they were good for.

As for modern poetry books, their words are sharp, and their gates do not yield to me; they do not yield with one reading, or even ten. Words—fortresses that do not open their gates to me despite all my assaults on them. They are smooth and hard. I had given up trying to befriend them, so I don't regret parting with them.

I came back home to find my sister arranging the

scattered books; she was not upset this time, she only smiled at me when I came in—a strange smile. I told her not to bother putting my books back in place because I was going to get rid of another bunch the next day. I was going to arrange the rest in a careful, final way. She shrugged and left. I think my sister is giving up on me and her old admiration is seriously wearing thin.

Tonight, too, the phone rang at a late hour, and when I answered, nobody spoke. I don't know if this was because there was trouble with the phone lines or if it was a prank, but this has been happening a lot around midnight.

Friday, July 31, 1986

I finished arranging my books today. I put all the books I no longer need in boxes and gave them over to the public librarian. I only kept the general knowledge books. I gave away all the autobiographical writings and the novels, even the history books, except *The History of Tears, The Encyclopedia of Weapons before Firearms,* and *The Glossary of Greek Mythology.* I shelved these reference books along with *The Glossary of French Law,* dictionaries in several languages, and reference books, even *The Glossary of Dream Interpretations,* and a small English dictionary of shoe manufacturing terms. I kept the neat copy of Ibn Hazem's *The Ring of the Dove: A Book on Love and Lovers* and squeezed it next to *What We Should Know about Military Aircrafts* and Arabic grammar books including a series of school books for intermediate level classes, and I got rid of *A Thousand and One Nights.* So all I kept were reference books. Today I think reference books make me feel secure, while the other books make me vulnerable. The dictionary organizes the world, and the novel turns it to rubble.

At around three, I went to visit Lutfi in his projection room at the movie theater where he stays for the whole time the movie is running. I will try to convince him to find M.F.'s picture for me.

I've kept away from Cinéma Royale, too. I check out what movie Al-Bahri is showing, but I avoid going in. For more than two weeks there has not been one single movie that would be harmless, except one. When I went into Lutfi's projection room, he asked me why I haven't been coming. "I can't bear watching movies anymore," I replied. I think Lutfi concluded from what I said that I didn't like the movies he was showing, and he agreed with me that Najib al-Bahri picks movies randomly, with no regard to their quality.

As he rolled his film, Lutfi was looking out from the little square window overlooking the street and enjoying the sight of the people, the passing cars, and the small restaurant with red curtains. The sixty-year-old owner, who is still obviously beautiful, serves the customers with her own hands. She's neat and clean; she drinks coffee with her daughter, and they scrutinize the passing people and whisper quietly. There is a floor above the restaurant; the white paint on the iron railing of its balcony is spotted with rust, and the windows are always closed. If Lutfi comes close to the window and looks left, he can see a part of our house across from him, and if he looks right, he can enjoy watching the sunset color the distant hill covered with olive trees where the ancient brick house stands alone.

Lutfi has worked for years in that cold room full of posters and movie-reel boxes. It has no furniture except for one chair, and a mirror, and a photograph of the young man who ran the projector before he did—his hair well combed and his eyes dreamy. Talking to Lutfi is always interesting because he reads a lot of books and magazines, even though he hasn't been to college. Today, he wanted to tell me about some new ideas like "the East is the original homeland of spirit and wisdom, and if anything of great importance were to happen, something that would dress the whole world in a new gown, it would definitely have to happen in the East."

Every time I visit Lutfi in his projection room, I sit on a stack of movie reel boxes, and he tells me about dates and battles that changed the course of history and great people who embodied the spirit of the East and all its wisdom. Lutfi has to raise his voice over the rattling of the projector, and he only stops talking when the audience starts shouting and whistling because of some glitch that's stopped the sound or made the picture fuzzy. And today, he stopped talking when a wedding procession passed by and the cars honked; he looked out of the window and saw the restaurant owner's daughter laughing and showering the bride and groom with handfuls of rice. Lutfi told me that he had gone into the restaurant several times and eaten lunch just to see her up close and maybe talk to her and that he managed to get her attention, but she kept up a front that made him lose all hope of ever getting better acquainted. However, when she glances toward his window every now and then, every time she lifts her head in his direction—knowing that he is here although she can't see him in the darkness of his projection room—he feels the need again to make another move to get to know her. I know this girl well, and today I enjoyed looking at her from Lutfi's window. I noticed she has a special charm—her milky complexion, her chestnut hair that she gathers up in a way that makes her neck look bare and sexy.

Lutfi returned to his projector and explained to me that while the West took over the East once, the East conquered the West twice and that this exchange is not over yet and will not be over. I was agreeing vaguely and offering simple remarks that were enough to encourage Lutfi to declare that the Jews have returned to the East and have established the State of Israel in order to fight the Christians and not the Muslims. He also confirmed that St. Paul is responsible for turning Christianity into a Church and drowning it in the mud of life.

Since Lutfi joined Brother Shafiq's group, his work at Cinéma Royale has been causing him a conflict of conscience, especially the evening shows. The owner of the movie theater, Najib Al-Bahri, has been working very hard to keep what few customers he still has. For that purpose, he has been slipping in a number of porno-graphic clips into the evening shows, until one of the priests got word of it and dedicated an entire Sunday ser-mon to Al-Bahri's behavior. So he was forced to stop showing these clips for a while. But he brought them back in and made a pact with his evening customers who swore to keep it a secret. They all knew each other, and if they were ever suspicious of one of the newcomers, one of them would go up to Lutfi's projection room and warn him to "clean" the movie because a "foreign bird" was in the theater. On those evenings, the show would end in a sad silence without the usual giggles or dirty cracks; snoring would be heard from some of the seats, and some customers would prefer to sneak out and spend the evening playing backgammon, "the dog's bone" as they call it, or watching the baccarat game in the café adjacent to Cinéma Royale. Lutfi told me that everyday he says a special prayer for God to forgive the sin that he couldn't avoid because of his desperate need for work.

When Lutfi mentioned St. Paul, I took the opportunity to ask him about their group and what had happened to them. He hesitated and then told me he hadn't gone with them to Ain Jawz because he had to work, and besides, he didn't believe a man needed any intermediaries between himself and God.

When I said goodbye to Lutfi, he asked me why I needed the picture of M.F. I smiled and didn't answer. He asked me whether I was okay, whether I needed his help or the help of his friends, and I thanked him. I am not okay, but how did it show, and how did Lutfi know?

Monday, August 3, 1986

Day after day, I become more picky about the eating rituals that I have forced on my mother and my sister. My day has gradually started to organize itself around these three meals—since I so far have managed to get them to sit down for breakfast, even if only at the kitchen table. In return, I have started to get out of bed early, before seven-thirty. This was their condition. Today, my sister said that she has started to get used to this system and that she will never give it up from now on. My mother is the only one who is obviously reluctant to give in to me, and I sometimes feel that her obedience to my rules is out of pity for me.

I stood at my bedroom window and looked out to the city port. Every time I watch the sea from my room, I get the writing fever. Crowded cities and pale women, like dreams, start flooding into my mind, and I remember the lilac bush and keep to myself.

Friday, August 7, 1986

After breakfast, I left for the café. I walked toward Al-Midan Square, as if every step I took and every bend of my body were being watched. When I got there, the broad-shouldered young painter was setting up his easel to the right of the square, opposite the only hotel in town. He set up his easel and stared at the horizon for a few minutes, his arms crossed. That's the way it is every time he comes to the square—he rolls up his sleeves and starts to outline hilltops and slopes. He blends earth blue with pomegranate red, and so the bottom of the painting is all purple and the top is sky blue. He comes nearly twice a week; people gather around him asking him questions, and he answers that these mountains are the original land—a land with no superstitions—and that he will never get tired of painting it. Then they disperse, smiling, also looking toward the tall, barren hills.

My gaze swept around the square. The old shoe-shine man was reading yesterday's newspaper while he waited for customers, the waiter at the café was using a pocket knife to carve the name of the girl he loves on the bark of the tree on the opposite side, the man selling corn on the cob was angrily lighting a fire, and the scrap-iron peddler was taking his morning nap. The laborers were sitting in a row, hoping for work, and the children were throwing pebbles in the round pond and splashing water at each other. I felt comfortable with this routine and walked, head down, hands clasped behind my back, my steps confident, to the last table by the wall of the café. I sat and let my body relax and my eyes wander.

The movement at Al-Midan is regular. It's enough for someone who is as familiar with the café as I am to raise his eyes a little in order to know that the group of giggling young women is deliberately passing by here and the old woman who is hastening her steps is late for the nine o'clock mass, and the retired school teacher, standing at the opposite corner, comes here just for the sake of coming to the square.

I straightened up and settled back in my favorite

sitting position. I stayed rigid and straight in the same position for an hour, an hour of distress and emptiness during which Al-Midan Square maintained its daily routine until Uncle Mansour suddenly appeared. He was walking toward me and looking in every direction except mine. I invited him to sit and have a cup of coffee, but he remained standing until I remembered that he does not sit with his back to Al-Midan. I stood up and offered him my seat, where he could lean his back to the wall, and I sat across the table from him. In no time he started to attack as he does every time we meet, "They say you're making your mother and sister sit down to formal meals every day," and before I could answer, he added, "The neighbors have been whispering about your behavior for a while. Be careful." I didn't want to argue with Uncle Mansour about this matter, so I only smiled like someone who was aware of what was happening around him. He rose from his chair and said as he was getting ready to leave, "I didn't like the way your uncle Rafael looked when he came to offer his condolences at your grandmother's funeral; he looked soft and flabby. Why doesn't he take better care of his health?"

After Uncle Mansour left, I sat there for about fifteen minutes, trying to recover my equilibrium and the rigidity of my body because our short conversation had tired me.

Then my friends started to come one after the other, and after a few words about this and that, the conversation went back to what it had been about every day for a week, the disappearance of Rasheed Abu-Samra. It is a mystery which the people of our town will talk about daily until it is solved. It seems to be the first time that something like this has happened, and nobody knows who is responsible for it. It might happen or have happened before, for example, that some fugitive from justice has been accused of an additional crime, but it would be a trick that only the judge falls for, not the people of his town. But the disappearance of Rasheed Abu-Samra, or his kidnapping as some are saying, is something troubling, very troubling. All the incidents that we or our parents have lived through, all the challenges, the shootings and the assassinations, all of these had clear and known motives, and the people committing them did not deny responsibility for them, even if they did try to hide from the law. That's why people who weren't involved in the circle of revenge or the game of political power used to know that they were in no danger at all. Rasheed Abu-Samra is one of those; his is among the few new families in town; they've been here only a hundred years; he doesn't have an extended family or relatives. So how would he have enemies, a hard working honest carpenter? His wife used to prepare his lunch because he ate early and did not wait for his sons to return from their jobs. A car stopped in front of the door of his house and a man called him by his name. His wife had not heard the voice before and didn't recognize it. So, Rasheed went out and she stayed in the kitchen. When she heard the car starting out again, she expected to see him coming back in to finish his lunch, but he hasn't returned. None of his neighbors or the passersby saw the car. Everyone keeps saying every day now that Rasheed is a happy and contented man, a good man, no one could possibly want to hurt him—an absolute mystery that no one has come up with an explanation for. If Rasheed Abu-Samra doesn't reappear, if he is found dead, as his wife and neighbors fear, it would be the worst thing that's ever happened in our town. It's true that there are a lot of animosities here, but we know our enemies; at least we know who they are, and we can rest.

When our meeting broke up around noon, and I left the café and Al-Midan, the broad shouldered painter was still coloring the distant mountains and the clear blue sky.

Monday, August 10, 1986

I started to make friends with my face again. Since I shaved my mustache, I haven't been able to look at it closely. I shave my face every day in front of the mirror, but I don't look at it; I don't examine it closely. My mustache used to divide my long face. In the United States, I sometimes used to twirl it up, and my friends would laugh, especially Lara, who used to tell me, I didn't have to show all the signs of my Eastern masculinity at once. Yesterday, I survived ten minutes in front of the bathroom mirror, so I discovered the blackheads on my forehead and nose, and I tried to squeeze them out, but it was a difficult task. I think there is a cream that gets rid of them; I will buy it at the drugstore and use it out of sight of my mother and sister. Today, I looked at my face for a while, long as it is, after I shaved my beard: I think I'm starting to accept it this way, instead of with the traditional part of my hair to the left, which lets a strand fall on my forehead. I don't like the strand anymore; it makes me look hesitant, pretentious; it hides my face. I think I will comb my hair back and have it cut very short so that the part will naturally disappear.

In the afternoon, I met Mary. Her summer vacation starts today and extends till the beginning of September. Mary works very hard, and the bank manager has been depending on her more and more lately. He has told her that he might interrupt her vacation and ask her to come back, if he has to. She's been working overtime, sometimes, it seems, and has been training the employees on the computer system the bank has recently acquired. Mary says that after living in the capital and meeting various people, she doesn't like the town and its atmosphere anymore, but she is forced to escape back here sometimes when the fighting starts and everything is tense and dangerous. Anyway, I am her only connection to town besides her parents; she comes in order to see me and says that she loves me, especially that she finds my company very entertaining. I understand everything Mary says about our relationship except that she finds my company entertaining. I have gotten this compliment from several friends before, and now when I count my merits to myself, and this is a rare thing, I include being entertaining among them, based solely on the testimony of others. The strange thing is that Mary says this, although we don't talk much during our dates. But I have to believe her. And this time, as well, we didn't talk long, although we had lunch together at the mill, which the owners have transformed into a fancy restaurant crowded with servants and different kinds of creative appetizers. I think that Mary noticed a change in the way I ate because she was staring at me the whole time. Many people have been staring at me these days, as if they were seeing me for the first time.

As we were leaving the restaurant, she told me she felt as if she were in the company of a different person.

I smiled, and she said she thought I'd been acting that way because I didn't love her anymore. This is her usual tactic to push me to prove the opposite. But today I couldn't do that. We started driving back, silent. I felt I didn't want to break that silence, ever. I didn't drive along our usual route. Mary asked me to take her back home. She is strong and didn't want to cry.

Saturday, August 16, 1986

Mary cut her vacation short and decided to go back to the capital this evening. She says her manager called her in because work has been a mess in her absence, and the employees have been making mistakes constantly. I didn't believe her and thought that she wanted to stay close to the manager, especially now since we've been growing further and further apart. She called today, saying she had to go back to the bank, and she waited for my reaction. She's putting me on the spot, and I don't feel like being diplomatic anymore. I won't allow her to make me take one single step that I don't want to take. When she said she was going back to work, I was supposed to be disappointed and ask her to stay, or to come back soon. But I didn't. I didn't even ask her to call me as soon as she came back, or tell her I'd drop by her place if I went to the city, as I used to do whenever we parted.

I'm not sure of my feelings toward Mary anymore. I love the quiet moments we spend together. I love sitting with someone who is quiet and calm—in a mutual self-contentment. For a long time, I've had this picture from the Degas painting, *L'Absinthe* stuck in my mind; it's of two people sitting together on the same bench and looking in a different direction. Together with other paintings such as *Ophelia Floats on the Pond like a Lily Pad*, *L'Absinthe* decorated the French literature book we used in secondary school. In Degas' painting, a man and a woman sit on the same bench at a café, two glasses of absinthe in front them, and their eyes wandering, as if Degas wanted to capture the emptiness of eyes and souls—I don't really care because there is really a fine line between stupidity and insight, and I can't tell anymore if I am predisposed to this kind of reflection or I'm recreating *L'Absinthe,* with me as the messy-haired man and Mary the woman who looks like a housemaid, sitting together in silence as we used to at Chez Paul when we first started seeing each other. Back then infatuation with her had made me follow her to the city, and we'd meet for lunch at that restaurant overlooking the sea. And so now I feel obliged to kiss her when we're alone and to keep telling her I love her. I can't take it any more. I wish that Mary would go to the capital and not come back.

Tuesday, August 18, 1986

I finally visited Uncle Rafael. He was sitting in his usual place on the balcony, wearing his comfortable *abaya* and holding a skein of yarn for my aunt to wind into a ball. He seemed to be observing the process with great interest, but when he saw me come in, he stood up to kiss me, and my aunt grabbed the yarn from him so it wouldn't get tangled. She let it rest on the back of a chair and continued winding the ball.

His breath smelled of garlic. My aunt probably doesn't smell it anymore. It's just unbearable. I almost cut my visit short because of it. He greeted me with enthusiasm and showered me with praise, saying that I'm smart and well read. As he spoke, he would look at my aunt sometimes, and she would smile, as was her habit when anyone addressed her. And as usual, my uncle started his clichés like, "There are two kinds of men who can't see: those who are blind, and those with no brain," or "All things in moderation." My uncle is trying to prove to me that he reads, too, that he is not a stranger to what he thinks is my world, the world of literature and ideas, and especially of eloquence. And perhaps to prove to me that he was well read, he stood up, went into the house, and came back with a small leather bag that looked like a school bag. Then he fell comfortably into the chair with all his fat, which his *abaya* didn't manage to hide, set his bag on his knees, opened it, and took out *Nahjul Balagha,* (The way to eloquence), by Ali bin Abi Taleb. As he handed me the book with his right hand, the leather bag fell over, and some of its contents scattered onto the floor, so my aunt rushed to pick them up because my uncle couldn't lean over because he's so huge.

A lot of things poured out of the bag. I only remember picking up a small round mirror, a comb, a picture of St. Sebastian with an arrow through his chest, two lottery tickets, about four keys of different sizes and shapes, several postage stamps, some hard rock candy, and a photograph of two wrestling stars with their arms around my uncle's shoulders, showing their love and happiness, one wearing a black mask and the other with the frame of a giant with his long hair loose and a chain around his neck. My aunt gathered up some of the things, too, and my uncle put everything back in the bag, quickly and haphazardly, closed it and mumbled some vague words, as if apologizing or making excuses for all those things in his bag. As he squeezed *Nahjul Balagha* into the bag, grabbed the bag, and was preparing to go in and take it back inside, I spotted something that we had missed on the floor next to the wall. I walked over and picked it up—a lock of blond hair wrapped in a crimson ribbon. When I asked my uncle if this was his, he mumbled again, but I realized that he was eager to tuck it away with the rest of his stuff.

He kept standing there in the doorway as if he didn't want to go in without this lock of hair.

Anyway, when he went back into his room, I noticed a notebook and pencil on the small table by his chair. I opened the notebook to page one: my uncle must have been making up a big crossword puzzle, full of women's names—I think they are the names of women he's loved—along with some interjections and a lot of connecting words to fill in the little spaces.

When I got back home, my sister told me Mary had called from Beirut, and she wanted me to call her back urgently. Mary can't accept what's going on with us, and she must be very upset and needs to vent her anger on me. I can't go into this labyrinth again—my relationship with Mary. I have decided not to call her and I told my sister, "If Mary calls again, tell her I got the message."

Friday, August 21, 1986

I changed my mind about getting my hair cut. Instead, I decided to comb it back and get rid of the part even though my face will look longer that way. Yesterday, I bought gel at the drugstore to keep my hair in place, and I bought a facial wash. I placed those two tubes over the sink next to the toothpaste and the razor. I hesitated a bit and thought about hiding them in my cabinet so that my sister wouldn't see them and start interrogating me, but I decided to keep them over the sink on purpose, since, sooner or later, I will have to face my mother and sister. So why try to be secretive and elusive now?

My sister noticed the two tubes yesterday. She didn't ask me about the hair gel, but this morning, as we were having breakfast, she asked me about the facial wash and if I knew how and when to use it. I guess my sister has stopped condemning me and disapproving of my behavior. She's worried about the way I've been acting, too. But I haven't hurt anyone. So why did my mother send for my aunt, the one she's never been very fond of, why did the aunt come shrouded in mourning clothes, hurrying in as if something were gravely wrong, and why did those two lock themselves in the kitchen for some heated discussion? What are they discussing? Me? Why? Because I want us to eat our meals regularly? Because I've given some of my books away to the public library? Or because, as they keep saying, I can't find a well-bred, nice woman to marry? I plan on doing other things they won't like.

I am trying to comb my hair back using gel. It's taking me a couple of tries to get my hair slicked back. I've been standing in front of the mirror for a long time since I got used to my face again, scraping the comb through my hair and watching. Why don't I just admit it?

Everything I try to do is in some way to get Lara's admiration. Even in choosing a hairdo, I look at myself with her eyes. Where is Lara these days? Did she move to Greece? Did she get married? Where is she right now, while I'm writing down these thoughts in the notebook that she gave me before I left? Where is she now, at four in the afternoon, on this day in the middle of summer and all these days zipping by as if they are racing toward the edge of a cliff?

Monday, August 24, 1986

Sitt Emily, the mayor's wife, returned from Brazil without prior warning. She didn't send a letter or any other notice that she was coming back. Nirmal came over and told us, in English, how she arrived in a cab and how he rushed to help her carry her suitcases to the front door. Nirmal hadn't known her before because he came after her sudden trip to her sister's. But he'd heard a lot about her. He said he could tell by her beauty and her fancy dress that it was her. She knocked at the door several times, then waited. Nirmal remained close to see what was going to happen next. In about five minutes, the mayor opened the door, but he didn't say a word and went back in calmly, and closed the door behind him. Sitt Emily kept standing at the door, not moving, not calling anyone. Some kids gathered near the house; then a neighbor walked over and invited Sitt Emily to rest in her house, but she thanked her and kept standing there, waiting. Nirmal told us that then, from inside the house, the mayor started shouting things he couldn't understand. Some kids were laughing now; Sitt Emily started crying. The Indian added, in his special accent, that he didn't like watching scenes like that, and he wanted to leave. But as soon as he moved a few steps away, the kids started shouting and applauding, so he looked back to see that the mayor had opened the door and his wife had gone in. "That's better," Nirmal said.

Friday, August 28, 1986

I found the hat yesterday, a pale gray fedora hat with a black ribbon. It was sitting in the glass case with bottles of perfume and women's hats whose colors had faded or which were already out of date.

I wasn't looking for a hat yesterday, but I was walking as usual to the old neighborhood at sunset after I'd made sure to walk near the mayor's house hoping to catch a glimpse of Sitt Emily, even if only from a distance. I was reflecting on how much these places inhabit me, and I realized how everything I've read happens here; the musketeers have duels with their opponents on these narrow streets, and the fortress where Edmond Dantès spent his prison years is but Sheikh Farid's mansion—although the prison in the tale is high on an island in the middle of the sea. The fairies of *A Midsummer Night's Dream* appear near Masoud's windmill, and Nikolai Stavrogin meddles with things and weaves his conspiracies between the houses stacked on top of each other behind the church. As for Oriane de Guermantes, she lives on the second floor of St. Joseph's School, which is ornamented with arches. Even Aureliano Buendía's house is our same old house, adding to it—I don't know what makes me mention that—part of our neighbor's house. These characters left our neighborhood for good when I saw them on the movie screen. The movies would take them away for good. The Brothers Karamazov, for example, have all left since I once saw them at Cinéma Royale as Yul Brynner and Lee J. Cobb, fighting with and chasing Maria Schell. I was trying to count the surviving characters when I saw the hat.

The glass case was standing on its wooden legs in the middle of the pavement. Souad takes it out every morning to leave more space for the women inside the store. Every time I've seen Souad's store, it's been flooded with women. Since my childhood, when the school bus used to drop us just outside the neighborhood and I'd walk on this side of the street on purpose, the big wooden door open to the street has attracted my attention, but I could not walk in and mingle with the women's bodies in the midst of heaps of colored fabric and boxes full of buttons, so I would stand next to the glass case, looking at what's inside it. Dust has built a nest in its corners, and Souad exhibits in the case fancy items she wants to protect from people's hands; she has a little key and lock for it. I wasn't surprised to find the fedora in it, because Souad has always placed one man's item in the case, a tie, a shiny silk bow-tie that perhaps stayed for years in the middle of a group of earrings, rings, old baby powder boxes that have Chinese writing and drawings on them (that powder whose smell I knew well from my aunt's kisses). I used to stand in front of the case for a few minutes, stealing looks at the inside of the store—dark in the middle of the day and heavily fragrant with the scents of women and colored soft fabrics.

Yesterday, when I stopped by Souad's glass case and spotted the fedora, I was seeking the same ecstasy and hoping I could sink back in it after all these years. That was it, just as I wanted it. It was even in pale gray—my favorite color—but I didn't buy it because, like every other thing in my life, I needed a distance from it, some sort of stepping back before I take my next step.

On the way back, I stopped again, for a moment, next to the glass case in front of Souad's store. This hat suits me perfectly.

I think Souad noticed my repeated stops in front of her store because she walked toward the door as I moved on. She can't recognize me, now that the night has started to fall.

Mary called while I was out. For ten days, she's been trying to talk to me, and I have been avoiding her. I haven't been picking up the phone; I leave this task to my sister whom I've entrusted to always say I'm not at home. The problem is that my story with Mary hasn't been malleable for a while. It has become impossible to dress Mary in any gown but her own.

Sunday, August 30, 1986

Today I returned to Souad's store to buy the hat. She doesn't close her store on Sundays since she lives in a room in the back. The wooden door was wide open, the dim light outside adding to the usual darkness inside. Souad recognized me. She was sitting behind her table when I stepped into her store for the first time in my life. She stood up to welcome me and called me by my name, which surprised me a bit. She also asked me about my mother and added that she's a great woman. Souad has a coarse face, her hair is disarrayed, and her dress hangs loosely on her body. Her lack of femininity has always amazed me, she who earns a living from women's elegance. There was no one in the store, and I felt there was almost nothing to sell either. Maybe it has always been like this, but the darkness and the crowdedness always gave it depth and richness from the outside. Souad remembered how I used to sit on our old balcony, reading and writing, and how she used to motivate her children to follow my example.

When I told her I wanted to buy the hat, she said she'd caught a glimpse of me three days ago, looking inside the glass case; she said she'd bought this hat from one of the merchants in the city because Sheikh Farid, the jeweler, had been asking her for an American hat. He is about the only one in town who wears these hats, and Souad had placed the hat in the glass case, so that Sheikh Farid would notice it when he walked by the store. But ever since she bought the hat, he's disappeared from the neighborhood completely, and Souad was worried about his health. I felt that Souad was telling me all that about Sheikh Farid and the hat to make me tell her what I wanted to do with it myself. I wasn't prepared for the probability of this coming up because I'd assumed Souad didn't know me enough to make me explain why I was buying this hat. The only way out that I could think of was to smile showing I understood why Souad was surprised at my buying such a hat; I assured her at the same time that she'd never be disappointed in me.

She wouldn't let me pay for the hat, but I insisted

and asked her for a bag to hide it in; then Souad walked me out. I felt she wanted to say something, so I encouraged her with a wondering look, but she hesitated. Then, as soon as I had walked a few steps toward our house, away from the old neighborhood, she called after me. I looked back, and she said, "Give my best regards to your mother." I thanked her and she added, "God be with you."

I returned home, carrying the hat in a bag. I didn't know what to do with it. I am new to elegance, and I'd read in a French book that for a person to be elegant, he should start early. Until the beginning of this summer, or specifically until the day they cut down the lilac tree that Sitt Emily had planted in the late '60's, I'd considered elegance the business of other people, women, and for Sundays. And when I got to high school, my friends and I made transforming Sundays into ordinary days our unwritten agenda: No attending mass, no new shirt or even a clean one, and absolutely no ties—not even skipping the visit to the hotel's café where the juke box played the hit songs, and where cream-decorated sweets always gave color to the tables. As soon as we achieved this goal, we started to compete in declaring Sunday the most boring melancholic day of the week—because melancholy was the new religion we prided ourselves in, the fortress from whose high balcony we looked down on our parents and pitied their drive for hard work. And in the United States, where they sent me to major in mechanical engineering and from where I came back with a degree in the humanities, I objected more strongly to paying attention to one's looks and discovered how people fake sloppiness, especially those girls who claimed they neglected their appearances but were just naturally elegant.

When I returned after four years, I only took care in curling up my thin mustache, but I had to shave it a few months ago to avoid the wondering looks. That's how my objection to elegance drove me to become part of the fashion of the day, the no-fashion. It is easier for me to wear my jeans. I don't own all that many clothes and my wardrobe always looks kind of empty, a few pieces of clothing and the one pair of shoes or two at the most. I like to wear the same clothes every day and to only change into something else if my clothes become dirty, and I don't buy something new except after a whole argument with my mother and sister. I usually get so used to a sweater or a pair of pants that I don't give up on them until they are torn; I rely on them. And there are clothes I wear for a few days, but they don't grow on me, so I neglect them and my mother ends up giving them away to the poor.

I went into my room, closed the door behind me,

even though I'd stopped doing that, stood in front of the mirror of my closet, got the hat out of the bag, shook the thick dust off of it—hoping to clean it properly later on—put the hat on, tilted it a bit to the right, and started laying the foundation for my new elegance.

Tuesday, September 2, 1986

Yesterday when the laundry boy passed in front of the house, I called him. It's the first time that I called him myself because I wanted to send my winter suit for dry-cleaning. Narcissus crosses town in a small car every day, stops dozens of time to hand over the clean clothes and pick up the dirty and take them to the laundry next to Al-Midan Square. Narcissus doesn't knock on the doors but calls out for a member of the family, imitating Father Antoun's voice, or other voices that everyone in town would recognize. When he stops in front of our house, he calls my sister, imitating my grandmother's voice, a voice which has a certain tremble to it and which people tell me I've inherited. It used to take my sister a few seconds to realize that Narcissus was the one calling her, and not my father's mom, and she jokingly prayed that he would lose the tongue that called. About two weeks after my grandmother's death, Narcissus went back to imitating her voice when he called my sister, and he almost caused her to faint and her heart to stop the first time he did it.

I gave him the suit, but no sooner had he left than he was back again, holding out some papers that belonged to my grandfather, which he'd found in the inside pocket of the coat. He gave me the papers and was starting to leave again but I invited him to sit down and asked him whether people usually forgot things in their pockets when they sent their clothes to the laundry. He whistled, meaning they forgot a lot of things. I asked him for examples, but he laughed and said he was in a hurry today and he'd tell me about that later.

Again the devil of writing was visiting me. The minute Narcissus left, I started constructing a story in which you can acquaint yourself with people's intimacies and uncover their secrets by what they forget in their inside pockets and what a nosy laundry boy finds—he may return the money if he finds any, but he will keep the letters and similar stuff. A tempting idea, and I usually add a secondary spin of events which has nothing to do with the main conflict except that it happens at the same place perhaps and the same time, and I make a story out of the two, a story I don't start writing before I come up with a title for it.

It is the second time I've fallen onto a "fertile" idea since I've stopped looking for ideas, since I've decided to stop writing. The first time was when one of my old friends from school came by, one of the "devils" on the bus, who used to create chaos getting on the bus and off it, one of those who kept making fun of me for a long time after the physics teacher praised me saying, "The student has overcome the knight."

My friend came by a month ago and said he expected I was still superior in math because I was in school, and he said that I was the only one who could help him solve a very important problem. He refused to say any more before taking me to his place where he took me into a room with a very sophisticated radio which could be tuned to "anything and everything transmitted through waves," he said—the warriors' code, the army units, the exchanges between trade ships in the middle of the sea, and even private calls.

He turned his radio on and started tuning it, and it started giving all kinds of sounds. The noises continued for a few minutes before my friend could get the wave he was looking for. He asked me to sit down and wait. I realized that he wanted me there to decipher the symbols of some code. We waited for a long time and talked about school memories, and the wandering peddlers whose voices used to reach us inside the classroom, and the math teacher who used to sleep on very hot days hiding behind his glasses. Then suddenly the wireless gave us a clear woman's voice, quickly calling out some words and numbers like "yahwa's sea 13, Return 25 cigars . . ." I told my friend that we had to record the code by copying it on paper so I could think about it. He walked over to the table and grabbed a notebook in which he wrote down about ten pages of these words and numbers.

I took the notebook back home with me, and before plunging into deciphering these symbols, I got *The Secret Codes from Hieroglyphic Writing to Electronic Minds* out of my cabinet and looked through it again. That was the first book I'd needed since I rearranged my library. I worked on the code for more than an hour until I realized I was getting nowhere with it. I stopped especially because I was no longer eager to defend my reputation for solving tough mathematical and problems of logic.

But after I returned the notebook to its owner and apologized for failing to decipher its codes, I kept having the urge, for a day or two, to compose something out of this terrible interference of voices. Who is this woman whose voice I heard on the radio? What was she saying? Why does what she said have to be codes and not real words? How could all these sounds come together in my friend's room—the sounds of war, trade, and passionate love? Questions that took me back places I wanted to leave, forever.

Thursday, September 4, 1986

Narcissus brought back the suit from the laundry. He stopped mimicking my grandmother's voice after my sister poured out her anger on him. I didn't remind him that he'd promised to tell me about the things he usually finds in people's pockets.

I wore the suit and tried the hat on, but no chemistry sparked between the two although their colors matched. There's a difference between a new hat I'm still getting acquainted with and a suit coat I've been refusing to wear for two years now—and I don't give up, but it doesn't bring me any closer to elegance, even though the suit has just been dry-cleaned and ironed. If I am to base my new elegance on the hat I found in Souad's glass case, I should be looking among my winter clothes, and I don't have much to look at there. On another note, I'm prepared to walk around town with my new hat, no matter how much people gossip or how loudly Uncle Mansour complains and how seriously my mother and my sister worry. But at least I will wear it only in the proper season, on cold and rainy days. Sheikh Farid el Sayegh wears his hat all through the year, but he is an old man, and his hat always has a line of dry sweat because of the heat. So, I'll wait till the cold days start. Meanwhile, I'll be picking out the clothes, shoes and tie now, to be prepared for the winter. I've got to think of my elegance for the summer, too, and I find it to be a problem since our hot season is long and harsh during most years. I don't think I will be able to do much about it, though, because I have to wear a suit—a uniform—and maybe also a vest unless I choose to wear suspenders. I won't make a final decision before I make a tour around the shops in town. Tomorrow I'll stop by the bank and withdraw some cash, and very soon, I'll go to the city to "shop" alone. A new surprise for my sister and my mother.

Around nine in the evening, that is about an hour ago, we heard loud explosions from the direction of the refugee camp, and the horizon was burning. Following that, as usual, was the shooting in all directions and then the streaking shots from the antiaircraft machine guns, and also two bright bombs which exploded, and nobody could tell whether the Israeli airplanes had dropped them, or the soldiers fired artillery in defense. Then in a few minutes the light and the noise calmed down. Darkness filled the skies again, and the ambulance siren started. The raid was over. Now total silence reigns. Even the town seems to have suddenly hushed.

Friday, September 5, 1986

I ran into Mary today on my way back from the

bank. We saw each other from a distance, so she tried to avoid me at first and wanted to cross the street to the other side. But I called her and she stopped, waiting for me to get to her. She asked me impatiently and sharply, "What do you want?" I tried to calm her, but I read anger in her eyes, anger I hadn't seen in her throughout our relationship. I felt she was capable of stabbing me with words. I asked her about her work and her vacation that was interrupted, and she smiled cynically and said, "Why do you ask? You don't care about what happens in my life." Then she added, with a clear desire at vengeance and sarcasm, "All you seem to care about is fixing your hair and cleaning your face like a woman. Why don't you do your nails, too?"

She walked away from me and crossed the street. I believe love is like war: we only know how it starts, and nobody knows how it will end. Who would have said that my story with Mary would break into pieces this way and would scatter on the street in front of the town hall under a Winston billboard?

One of them, either my mother or my sister, found the hat out. I had put it back into the bag after I tried it on with the suit, without attracting anyone's attention, and then hid the bag in the back of my wardrobe. Today, when I went into my bedroom after lunch, I found it on my pillow on the bed. Anyway, the atmosphere has been very strange around our house lately. My mother and sister talk to me only about urgent business although we meet three times a day at the dining table. But my mother's sudden sighs are more frequent, expressing distress she can't let out. And she continues to have my aunt over—three or four times this summer—and consult with her about something, whispering in the kitchen, where my sister always joins them.

Monday, September 8, 1986

I work diligently on cleaning my face everyday. I've been making some progress and my skin is starting to look soft and shiny. Lutfi noticed it when he came over today, and he said my eyes looked bigger and more beautiful. He told me they would be showing a movie with an unusual title, *The Purple Rose of Cairo.* I said I'd go watch it. We discussed with Lutfi the disappearance of Rasheed Abu-Samra. No news about him, not even a clue as to what happened to him. The conversation shifted from the kidnapping, which always goes in an empty circle, to a new complication—the fact that a man is considered alive until death is confirmed—meaning, his wife and children can't inherit or sell the property.

Wednesday, September 10, 1986

I spent two days buying my clothes. I was shopping

like a bride before a wedding. Two days in a row, I went
to the city and into the stores—the store windows were
displaying summer clothes and beach wear. It was
Monday, the day before yesterday, just after lunch, and
the streets were almost empty because it's the month of
Ramadan and people are fasting. I asked about winter
clothes, and the store owners led me to a back room or
to the basement. I wanted to take my time choosing my
clothes because I realize how I usually have very little
patience: I buy the first thing I like because I'm embarrassed to leave the store without buying anything. I
always argued with my mother about that. This time I
didn't want to rush, and I understood the basic principle
women follow when they go shopping—and maybe
some men, too, but they don't admit it: when they buy
provisions for the winter, for example, they first go to all
the grocery stores; they ask about the prices and check
the quality; then they go back to where they found the
best kinds. That way a woman spends the whole morning shopping, but makes sure she's gotten the best prices.
Not because women love economizing, but because they
hate regret.

This time I couldn't afford regrets either. I was looking for a gray suit to go well with my fedora, and I found
it. Bluish gray. The young man who helped me try it on
said it's the latest fashion for the next winter, and when
I told him it reminded me of the thirties instead, because

of the coat's cut and the cuffs on the pants, he agreed that the new fashion designers are trying to imitate old-fashioned styles. I was surprised at the price; I guess keeping up my elegance is going to be very costly. My mission didn't end when I finally picked the suit I wanted. I'd intended to buy everything new—even underwear. And indeed, I didn't go back home until I'd bought a cotton undershirt and long underwear, which I'll make sure to hide from my mother and sister. I still had to buy a tie and a pair of shoes and socks the next day.

I bought the off-white shirt the day before yesterday when I bought the suit, and I already knew what type of shoes I like. They're called "Derby"—black wingtips. I also had to take care of the small details—the tie, the socks, and the suspenders. I spent all yesterday morning trying to decide on their colors.

My outfit is complete. I still need the gold pin for the tie. I should be able to find one among my father's things.

This afternoon I locked my bedroom door from the inside. (I wish my mother and sister would go visit somebody and leave me alone.) I tried on my new outfit. I stood in front of the mirror for a long time: I am ready. Tomorrow or the day after, I will go to "Al Sharq Photography." One thing had me worried. When I fixed the tie and I put on the hat and tilted it a little in front of the mirror—and that was the final touch—the smell of garlic coming from Uncle Rafael came back to me.

I'm not exaggerating when I say that even today I can still recapture the smell of my grandfather on my father's side, who passed away when I was six—a blend of red soil recently hoed and of coarse pears. He used to hold me on his lap and slip me money behind my grandmother's back. I can't get the smell of garlic out of my head; Uncle Rafael keeps destroying the fresh, glowing image I have of him. It will take the place of the leather hat, lined with wool, which hangs down over his ears. The truth is that what I'm suspicious of, what I actually fear (and why wouldn't I?) is not the resemblance between the two of us—the similar facial features, color of the eyes, shape of the fingers and hands—but rather the numerous signs over the last few years, that have made me feel closer to his disposition. My emotional outbursts, the answers I'm always blurting out, my taking it easy on myself, and my failure to force myself to do anything, and above all a distressing impatience that's been making me want to run away without looking back, and a fear of being weak and useless. Signs of Uncle Rafael's character are growing in me. I won't be able to escape from them.

Thursday, September 11, 1986

I saw *The Purple Rose of Cairo* today. I had been reading some things about this movie and hadn't expected it to show in town.

I love Cinéma Royale. For a long time I've considered it a second home—since it was bought by Najib Al-Bahri, who keeps reminding me that we're relatives whenever I see him or walk up to the ticket window, and he keeps refusing to let me pay for my tickets, but I keep insisting till he backs down and accepts the money. The reason he gives for not charging me is that he and my mom's father are cousins and that when my grandfather emigrated to Venezuela he sent for him so that they could work together: "But I was a coward." I even felt more comfortable there when Najib Al-Bahri hired my friend Lutfi from our old neighborhood to run the projector after the guy who was in charge of it left for Cairo. That guy was handsome—always combing his hair with the comb he carried in his back pocket. He was always complaining about burying his future here. As soon as he got a chance, he left. Nobody knows anything about him now, but it's said that some people saw him in one of Fatin Hamama's movies, playing the role of her taxi driver. So, the people in the movie theater applauded for him, and they added his name, hand-written, to the name on the poster. I like going up to Lutfi's projection room. Every time I climb the wooden stairs to sit next to him on the movie reel boxes, my feeling of being superior to the others who are sitting in the darkness increases—sort of like the pleasure of someone who creates a myth and falls for it.

There was one poster on the board outside the movie theater. The poster only showed a young woman wearing a brown dress and looking quizzically toward a pale young man whose face and outstretched hand were all that appeared. I arrived at the movie theater at five to four. I argued a bit with Najib Al-Bahri about paying for my ticket, went up to Lutfi's room to say hello, then went down quickly to find a seat before the lights were turned off. The regulars were in their seats, and there were other customers as well. The movie's title, written in Arabic under the poster, must have attracted these people to it or reminded some of them of another movie, *The White Rose,* which, for the first time in town, had gotten the women into the movie theater, where a lot of tears were shed.

Lutfi turned off the lights, so Rabi applauded, and the movie started right away. It's been a while since Najib Al-Bahri has stopped showing previews of coming attractions, because he wants to save time. And because he isn't sure of the schedule for the next shows anymore. It soon became clear that the events of the movie didn't take place in Egypt, but in a small town in the United States. The movie started with a long dispute between a young woman with wide eyes and her drunken, gambler of a husband. Mr. Anees cleared his throat as a sign of dissatisfaction and fidgeted in his customary seat.

The dispute between the woman and her husband wasn't going anywhere. Then the movie took us to the restaurant where the woman worked as a waitress. She started a conversation with one of her coworkers. Mr. Anees fidgeted some more and moved his chair, which made a squeaking noise; then I guess he put away his glasses; then he put his hat back on, stood, said something, and headed toward the door mumbling. The heroine went out to the movies alone and took a front seat watching a black and white movie that had men and women in expensive party clothes and a young man, wearing a pith helmet and something like a boy scout uniform, and everyone was exchanging toasts and best wishes.

Suddenly a strange voice was heard from the center of the movie theater. We all listened and there he was, Rabi, barking like a dog, a French poodle—intermittent barking, and then mewing, too. Everyone burst out laughing, so Lutfi came down from his projection room, and we could hear him, scolding Rabi and threatening him to tell Najib Al-Bahri, so Rabi stopped making noises and the movie theater was calm again.

The woman with wide eyes managed to sneak out behind her gambling husband's back and return to the movies the next day to see the same black and white movie called *The Purple Rose of Cairo.* She sat in the same seat on the third or fourth row, in the middle. She was alone, passionately following the words and movements of the man, the scout, as he stood among his handsome male friends and the gorgeous ladies.

On the third day, she went back to the movies after she was fired by the owner of the restaurant because she'd been slow in serving the customers and had stumbled a few times as she served the pizza and the drinks to the tables. The movie theater was almost empty; the American town was small, and the movie had been showing for several days. She took her seat and passionately followed the events of the movie. Suddenly, the man—the scout—noticed that there was someone intently watching him, so he approached the front of the screen. He spoke to the woman, who didn't realize what was going on; then he jumped off the screen into the movie theater. He was in color.

Rabi applauded hard with his coarse hands and it was noisy again. Lutfi went down from his projection room again, and with the flashlight in his hand, he focused the light onto Rabi's head. Rabi made his huge body sink in the seat, and afraid, he stopped talking. During that time, Moussa got up from his seat to sit next to me. He must have watched me coming in to see where I'd sit, so he could come sit next to me when he needed to. And here's what happened: when the scout man jumped out of the screen, gained color, and escaped with the woman with wide eyes to the city streets, Moussa felt that he'd missed out on something. So even before he asked, I told him that the actor had walked out of the screen and become an ordinary man and had gone with the woman, and that his friends in the movie were complaining and demanding he come back because they couldn't go on with the movie without him, and they were now discussing amongst themselves what they should do and to whom they should complain . . . But Moussa interrupted me and asked how we were and whether we had sold any of the land my father had left us. And before I could answer, he asked me whether I'd gotten married. I tried to answer him and still watch the movie. Moussa lit a cigarette and started looking at the screen again. And he stopped asking me questions.

Moussa didn't stay there for more than ten minutes. He only stayed until the owner of the theater was insistently calling *The Purple Rose of Cairo* production company urging them to solve the problem because the movie couldn't go on till the man—the scout—returned. So the production company sent him the actor who played the role. When the actor showed up looking for his character, who had run away with the young woman, Moussa stood up, asked me to give his regards to my uncle Mansour, and left. In any case, when I looked at the seats behind me, I could only see Rabi, who had brought in a stack of old magazines with him and was holding them close to his face to see the pictures of the models in the dark.

The three of us remained there, Rabi, myself, and Aziz, who was in the front seat as usual and had fallen asleep during the first few minutes, no doubt. The woman met the actor and thought he was the scout, so he tried to convince her to get the character to go back to the screen, and in exchange he would take her to Hollywood. And here's what happened: the scout went back to the screen and lost his color, the actors were able to relax, and the movie could start again; and the trick worked on the woman with wide eyes, who ended up going to the movies every day hoping something similar would happen again.

The lights were turned on, and Rabi left, barking softly. I stayed in my seat for some time to wipe away the young woman's melancholy from my heart. I waited in the calm of the theater for Lutfi to come down on his usual round looking between the seats to make sure no one had left anything behind and to wake up Aziz, who had not been disturbed by any shooting or loud music today and was still sleeping deeply in the front seat. Lutfi was surprised to find me still sitting where I was. Thinking I was sitting there because I'd been bored, he said, "If Al-Bahri keeps getting these cheap, outdated movies, we'll lose the few customers we still have."

Aziz woke up before Lutfi got to him, and the three of us walked out. Lutfi locked the doors of the theater. I looked toward our house. My sister was sitting on the balcony as usual, knitting and probably listening to "Radio Love." In the light of the setting sun, the life I had ahead of me suddenly seemed like a field that I had to sow with my very own hands. But whatever happens, I won't go back; I will move ahead no matter what. I looked to the right: the breeze was making the two cypress trees embrace over on the hill covered with olive trees, next to the house perched on its own in the distance.

Friday, September 12, 1986

I don't think the photograph will turn out right. That's what always happens when you stand (or sit as I did today) in front of the photographer and feel that the moment the camera flashed wasn't exactly the right moment for you. Either you haven't focused at all, or you have focused for too long, and your thin fake smile is captured in the photograph. As for the nice photographer, he was amazed that after all the effort I'd taken and the time I'd spent, sitting and getting ready to sit, I asked for only one photograph. I didn't mind his taking many shots to make sure one would work out, but I told him I wanted only one photograph the size of a postcard. And when he asked me what I wanted him to do with the negatives, I told him I was ready to pay for any time he had devoted to me, as long as he gave me a flawless, successful photograph. But I don't think he wanted to charge me any extra; he seemed amused. He agreed that this type of portrait could only be taken in black and white because color, as he said, took away its charm. He even gave me some advice as to how to wear the hat and how to sit down, but I didn't take any of it because I'd spent a long time practicing how to sit down and place one hand on my waist, how to pull the coat a little bit back to show the suspenders and blow my chest up a little bit, and especially how to turn my face away from my body and keep my body straight and rigid—how to cross my legs so that a strip of my socks would show and how not to look straight at the lens but rather at a point next to it. I had decided on a "pose" in front of the camera which was not "natural" in any way, but one which I'd reached through infinite attempts to achieve the best look of elegance and manliness. I followed these steps to the letter because I'm sure that the art of posing for a picture is artificiality.

The eyes, the look, and what it conveys were still there, and this, too, comes with practice. But I still needed to think of something, to imagine myself in a certain setting, in front of my cousin in the pink shirt, who was torn by bullets, and his mother who instead of wailing over him, was singing the children's hymn

Why, why, my son
Two eyelashes on your cheeks
One from God, my son
And where's the other from?

I thought that if I retrieved this moment from my childhood and stopped at it, part of it would show in my eyes.

He took four shots, asking me to change the way I sat and the direction I looked every time; he even suggested I stand up and lift one foot onto the chair. But I refused to change anything I'd practiced. He kept looking at me, surprised, even when I took off the suit and the hat, and put them back in the bag, put my old shirt and pants on and left his shop, thanking him and apologizing for having given him trouble. He said the next day was Sunday, a holiday, so the portrait would be ready on Tuesday.

In the window front there was only one portrait in black and white, a portrait of a family, looking happy and in good health: a father and a mother and their son and daughter, smiling broadly. I couldn't imagine why they were smiling, but they must have agreed to do it.

Some families, escaping the horror of the battles in Beirut, arrived in our town. My sister told me she went with one of her friends to Al-Midan Square especially to see them, bringing in their cars whatever clothes or valuables they could save. They checked in at the hotel and looked exhausted. People circled around them, asking all sorts of questions. It seems that hell has broken loose. Unbelievable. They had to flee with their children. They all have children—big families except for one woman who didn't mix with the crowd; she had a young blonde daughter. They arrived in a dark red Honda and went straight up to the hotel. The woman had a suitcase, and the girl had a blonde doll that looked like her.

The phone rang again tonight. I picked it up, but no one spoke.

Monday, September 15, 1986

After dinner last night, Uncle Mansour came over. He called out to us instead of knocking at the door. As soon as he walked in, he asked my sister to bring him coffee, as a hint that his visit wouldn't be over quickly this time. My sister went into the kitchen and my mother tried to exit the room, thinking Uncle Mansour might want to be alone with me, but he insisted on her staying, stressing that there are no secrets between him and me, "Isn't that so, my nephew?"

We started talking about all sorts of things. We shifted from the olive harvest, which looks good and needs an early rain, to the dwindling number of marriages in the last few years, and I was waiting for the real subject that my uncle had come for since we had to guess, as usual, the reason behind his visit. Contrary to what we've come to expect from Uncle Mansour, he took part in the conversation from the beginning, though very succinctly, and using abstract phrases.

And suddenly, at some word that my mother said—I didn't notice what—he started talking, without any reason—contrary to his habit—as if he'd come over tonight especially to say all that. Uncle Mansour has never in his life spoken non-stop for a whole half-hour, and I think that today he talked as much as he had talked for a whole year. He was addressing my mother the whole time. True, there was no special reason for what he was saying, but it was clear he was preaching to someone, not my mother, of course. He rarely looked at me, and then only accidentally, but I understood the sermon was meant for me. He got so excited, he stood up a few times and was making hand gestures as he talked. I tried to interrupt him more than once to make him address me and take it easy on my poor mother, but he started all over again, addressing her by saying, "My sister-in-law, this land was not always ours; we took it by the sword. The soldiers would stake their claim on it by putting a stone under the berry they had set their heart on in our grandparents' land, and no one in town dared pick its fruits—not until Yusef Beik came and gave us our freedom. The bells of the Virgin's Church were made of wood because were forbidden to ring our own bells. And its doors—don't you wonder why our grand parents built them small and low—no one could enter through the doors unless they stooped down. So the Turkish soldier wouldn't be able to get into the church on his horse. This country has been paid for with blood. In 1929, we managed to get in the parliament by force; we snatched it from the mouth of the lion. The French army started shooting at the picket line in Al-Qubba. Salim Diab was shot and killed. When his wife knew he'd died, she started shouting out to the people: 'Keep going! He hasn't been hit. He just fainted and will wake up shortly.' The French commissioner and the mayor were afraid, and the soldiers didn't dare shoot anymore."

My mother was nodding her head in approval all the time; that was all she could do. But I think she understood what he meant. When she looked in my direction, I could read some pity on her blank face.

He brought back everything, all the stories that I know and that I've heard separately throughout these years, in our house and in the café, ever since the Mamluks besieged the people of the town in the Assi Hawqa cave, flooding it with water until they drowned—until we attacked Alhamadiyya and Bishop Joachim killed their leader at Jamm Barbees, and they scattered in fear. And he didn't forget the battle of Binshaya and how Butrus Tuma darted toward a Turkish canon that was shooting at Yusef Beik, and how his friends and Jindel took care of the soldiers near him, and he stretched his strong arms to grab him and lift him on his shoulders and took him back to join his friends. And when he got to them, a bullet hit him in the chest and he dropped dead. He also told the story of Al-Ghazal and Al-Akouri, who escaped from the soldiers of Al-Mutasarifiyya in Mount Lebanon and of how they trapped them at Al-Nawaheer Spring where Al-Ghazal kept fighting until he was out of ammunition and then broke his rifle and drew his sword, so the soldiers didn't dare come any closer but circled around him and emptied their rifles into him and killed him.

At least half an hour of stories of heroism and tragedy, which Uncle Mansour concluded by addressing my mother, just as he did when he first started, "And don't think we're done. The worst is still to come." Then he stood and apologized,

"But we've said too much already, and we've taken too long." Then he turned around and headed for the door, shrugging his shoulders and pointing as he always does, as if saying, "Don't say I didn't warn you. I'm not responsible for what happens next."

After Uncle Mansour left, the three of us remained silent for a while; then my mother told me, "He's right, you know; our life in this country has been and will be tough."

Thursday, September 18, 1986

I went to the photographer's studio. He laughed a little when he saw me and got out the picture, but before letting me see it, he asked if I'd let him put it up in his studio's window. I imagined my picture next to that of the smiling family and told him I needed the picture to send it abroad. He told me he'd treat it with Ciba, an old dimming chemical, because everything in it—my suit, the hat, the suspenders, and the manner of sitting . . . even my looks—goes back to the past. And he added that I reminded him of the first movies that used to come to town and that he didn't like the movies anymore because movies today have become full of ugly, short actors with shabby hair and flat feet. Then he said, pointing to my picture, which I was looking at attentively, "We don't see such good-looking people anymore."

He said that the photograph—he was talking about the photograph as if he weren't talking about me—also reminded him of the ministers of the first Government of the Independence, who visited the town hall, and he pointed toward the old town hall.

I paid him what I owed him and wanted to give him more, but he wouldn't take it. The portrait was exactly as I'd wanted it: one in which I didn't recognize myself. I stopped by a bookstore and bought a suitable envelope to put the picture in. I intended to send it with a letter, but when I saw the photograph, I changed my mind. I'd send it without a word, without an explanation. I wrote Lara's address in New York on the envelope and when I got to town, I went straight to the travel agency and asked its owner to send it. He promised to do his best.

My mother says the signs of winter are beginning to show. I don't care about that because I've completed my plan, and here I am, clean and elegant. My life is smooth and organized. I don't fear the rain or anything else.

Monday, September 22, 1986

The brightness of this morning was expected. It's the morning that follows the first rain, after a summer I thought wasn't going to end, because, like every year, I had gotten used to its blue sky and its snow-like patterns of clouds and then an unexpected light wind blows at noon—just as it did yesterday, Sunday—and it blows the yellow sycamore leaves in a hurricane so that the house-wives close their shutters, and the people on the streets close their eyes to avoid the dust. The wind gains speed, waking up the soil and the lazy emotions of the summer, scattering things around; then the old people ask for rain and it comes. Big slow drops, a few at a time, drops that clean the air and the streets and cause melancholy. The night comes from behind the barren hills, which the broad-shouldered painter is still watching, the hills he doesn't get tired of sketching and coloring. The night comes from behind those hills, the world sinks without a moon, and I am overcome by a weakness that has no hope except the promise of the next morning. I expect the next morning and it arrives. It rises slowly, allowing my body to get in tune with the atmosphere of the place, and I realize that the love of life might come to me from a bright sun and the smell of the soil. It is summer's revenge, a passing and final revenge. It is the autumn equinox, the equilibrium of the elements, the brilliant culmination of the summer.

I woke up early. I've been waiting for this day. I took a hot shower. I rubbed the soap skillfully over my head and over my body. I put on my new underwear and socks slowly and carefully. I shaved my beard clean and combed my hair back with gel. I wore my suit and took my time in front of the mirror to adjust the flowery red tie. I ate breakfast with my mother and sister. My sister laughed at the suspenders. And when I stood again in front of the mirror to put on my hat and leave, my mother stopped me saying, "Do you want people to laugh at us? Why this hat?" I smiled, kissed her forehead and walked out of the door. Everything was perfect. The only thing missing was that my new shoes didn't squeak. I tried hard to get them to, but I couldn't. It must be the type of leather the sole is made of. In spite of that, I still tried to press my feet hard on the ground as I crossed the garden toward the road, hoping to create a noise.

As I walked in front of Cinéma Royale, eyes began to follow me. The sixty-year-old restaurant owner and her daughter kept staring at me. The barber greeted me loudly from afar—although he usually doesn't. I flaunted around, casting a quick look at the store windows and even the car windows to catch a glimpse of myself. I was nervous because of my hands—I didn't know what to do with them. They suddenly became a burden. I met Nirmal next to the building where he works, and he gave me a broad smile and whistled to say he was impressed. I found a way to solve the hand problem. I placed them in my pockets and started walking with my eyes fixed on the far away hill covered with olive trees. I passed by the mayor's house and walked down toward St. Joseph's School; I was walking aimlessly—more pushed forward than actually walking. The only plan I had was to take turns that wouldn't make me look lost and wandering aimlessly. When I passed St. Joseph's School I said to myself, "I'll go to church," or that's what a person who saw me was supposed to think. And when I took the curve around the church and didn't go in, to avoid the narrow street where Souad's store is, I pretended to be going home, one hand in a pocket and the other playing with my tie. I kept walking around for half an hour, full of myself, walking and not thinking of anything, clean, happy. And then when I started to feel tired and noticed I'd be walking the same streets again soon, I headed toward the café in Al-Midan Square.

I got there earlier than usual. None of my friends were there yet. The shoe-shine man stared at me curiously. I don't know why I was panting, but I hurried to my usual chair at the last table next to the wall. I sat down, looking for the waiter. I needed a cup of coffee. Al-Midan Square was quiet; the corn-on-the-cob vender wasn't there yet. I noticed the woman the moment I sat down. She was carefully coming down the hotel stairs, paying attention to where she placed her feet, her body leaning to one side, as she held on tight to a black handbag. When she got to the bottom of the stairs, she stood for a second, tightened her grip on the bag, and walked toward the square. I assumed she was going to walk across the square to the market like the other hotel guests who walk back slowly carrying bags of grapes and blushing green apples. She was walking with small calculated steps, her eyes steady, not examining the place the way the usual hotel guests do on the first day they arrive, or the way strangers do when they get off the charter bus and only get back on when the driver calls out, reminding them that they have a long schedule ahead.

She got to the round pond and traced her steps back—without any warning. It looked as if she had forgotten her wallet in her room, but she didn't show any sign of forgetting. She didn't check her bag or move her hand; she didn't hesitate. She even made an about-face as if she were following a path she'd already planned, one she began when she started at the top of the stairs, and here she was returning to the first step and climbing it carefully, her body leaning forward and her hand holding her black handbag tightly, as she disappeared into the dark lobby of the hotel.

The café was still empty, even the waiter wasn't around. He was probably inside. Al-Midan Square was empty, except for the shoe-shine man, reading a newspaper, and some yellow sycamore leaves from yesterday's storm, piled up in the corners and here and there on the chairs.

She left the dark lobby a second time; she went down the stairs, carefully taking every step, her eyes following her feet, discovering the stone steps as if she hadn't walked on them a few minutes ago. She stopped again at the bottom of the stairs, not hesitating—the movements of her body were smooth, no delay and no pause. She didn't lift her eyes, didn't look around her, as if she knew Al-Midan Square by heart. She walked toward the square another time, but she didn't take the right side down; rather she walked from the other side toward the old shoe-shine man. The sycamore trunk blocked my view of her, so I moved my head to follow her on the other side, but she didn't show up. She traced her steps back, the same steady and small steps, toward the stairs and walked up, perseveringly and carefully, and disappeared into the hotel.

I felt something was going on, and I couldn't comprehend it all. The waiter came out from I don't know where. He looked at me and laughed. He was happy and said he didn't recognize me, that with the suit and hat he thought I was one of the hotel guests. I asked him about the woman, and he told me it had been more than a week since she had come in with her daughter, and he thought that she was running away from the fighting in the capital. The news broadcasts had been reporting heavy bombing and unprecedented fires.

I asked the waiter for a cup of coffee and was getting ready for my friends and their questions when the woman came down the stone stairs for the third time. Behind her this time was a young blonde girl, her hair in a single braid down her back; she was carrying a doll in her hand and moving forward, trying to stay within the small circle of the mother's shadow. It was the woman my sister had told me about. This time she walked toward the entrance of the café, where she stood for a minute, and then she came in. I think I tightened my facial muscles. She sat at that table in the middle of the café. She turned her back to me and pointed to her little girl to sit on the chair facing her. I relaxed a little bit. She sat in the café just as the many hotel guests sit, some of them insisting on smoking their morning Arguila and others entertaining themselves with a book from their bags.

I didn't hear her voice. She probably ordered herself a cup of coffee with a whisper, forcing the waiter to lean forward to hear her. The little girl didn't order anything; she sat, the doll in her lap—it really looks like her. Her legs were dangling from the chair, not touching the ground, and she was swinging them rhythmically. She stared in the woman's face. The woman was hunched in on herself, as if she were clutching to her body the black leather bag with three shiny buttons in her lap. When the waiter got her the coffee, she took a sip and put the cup back onto the table, leaving a lot of lipstick on the rim.

Suddenly the little girl found me out. She stared at me. I moved my eyes away toward the pond then looked again. The girl stopped swinging her legs as she was looking at me with doubled curiosity, hugging her doll. She kept staring, so I tried to distract myself from her by observing the rhythmic movements of the shoe-shine man. She turned to her mom, and I knew she was going to ask about me. I felt a tremor, but she said, "What are you looking at, Mom?" She didn't answer her. Her head didn't budge. She had short fine brown hair. As if she were not expecting an answer, the little girl was staring at me again, and a beginning of a smile was on her face, or maybe I imagined it. She went back to her mother.

"What are you looking at, Mom?"

There was no impatience or sharpness in her question. The mother didn't move. But at the third question, "What are you thinking about, Mom?" I noticed the woman huddle into herself more; her hands drew closer to each other, and she bent her back a bit. My nerves were on edge, and I kept looking around in all directions. The little girl's questions were knocking hard at my heart's door. I was scared. "Why don't you cry, Mom?"

I stood up from my chair, ducked my head between my shoulders, and I hurried to the café door. I crossed Al-Midan Square fast, like someone crossing a battlefield in view of the enemy.